ZEPHYRZ
BY GARTH TOXO

Zephyrz

Garth Toxo

Published by Am I Am, 2024.

This is a work of fiction. Similarities to real people, places, or events are entirely coincidental.

ZEPHYRZ

First edition. August 2, 2024.

Copyright © 2024 Garth Toxo.

ISBN: 979-8227384348

Written by Garth Toxo.

In the distant future, humanity has transcended the boundaries of physical reality, creating a vast digital universe known as the Hyperverse. This immersive virtual reality realm, accessed through a sleek and sophisticated vapor device, offers limitless possibilities and adventures.

Our story begins as a mysterious entity, cloaked in shimmering light, materializes at the entrance of a new level within the Hyperverse. The entity, known as Zephyr, takes a deep breath, the vapor device seamlessly connecting to their consciousness. With a single step, Zephyr enters the new realm, ready to explore and uncover the secrets that lie within.

The environment shifts around Zephyr, morphing into a landscape of surreal beauty and intricate detail. The air hums with an otherworldly energy, and the vibrant colors pulse with life. Zephyr surveys the surroundings, their senses heightened by the Hyperverse's immersive technology. The journey has just begun, and countless challenges and wonders await.

Zephyr moved cautiously through the strange and shifting landscape of the Hyperverse. The world around them was an ever-changing mosaic of colors and shapes, a dreamscape that defied the ordinary laws of physics and logic. Here, reality was malleable, a canvas for the imagination. Yet, beneath this ethereal beauty, Zephyr sensed a hidden order, a code that governed the very fabric of this digital universe. This code, known universally across the cosmos, was the foundation upon which all virtual realms were built, a shared logic that transcended the boundaries of space and time.

Zephyr was not alone in this understanding. Aliens from another dimension, beings of pure energy and intellect, had long mastered this universal code. They were the Architects, creators of worlds and shapers of realities. Their existence was intertwined with the Hyperverse, their knowledge woven into its very essence. It was said that the Architects could bend the code to their will, manipulating the digital fabric to create wonders beyond human comprehension.

As Zephyr ventured deeper into the Hyperverse, they encountered traces of these alien entities. Strange glyphs and symbols, incomprehensible to most, but to Zephyr, they were faint echoes of a language they were beginning to understand. The air crackled with energy, the environment responding to Zephyr's presence, as if acknowledging a kindred spirit.

Among the many secrets whispered within the Hyperverse, there was one that intrigued Zephyr the most: the existence of a system known as "Rising." Legends spoke of Rising as a realm within the Hyperverse, a place where the boundaries between dimensions blurred, and where the true power of the universal code could be harnessed. It was said that those who mastered Rising could unlock abilities far beyond the capabilities of ordinary beings, transcending even the limits of the digital and physical worlds.

Zephyr's quest was clear. They needed to find Rising and uncover its secrets. The journey would not be easy, for the path to Rising was guarded by the most intricate and challenging puzzles, designed by the Architects themselves. But Zephyr was determined, driven by an insatiable curiosity and a desire to understand the true nature of the Hyperverse.

Navigating through the shifting landscape, Zephyr encountered a series of gateways, each guarded by a unique puzzle. The first gateway was a labyrinth of light and shadow, where the path forward could only be revealed by aligning beams of light in a specific pattern. Zephyr studied the glyphs around the entrance, deciphering the clues left by the Architects. With careful precision, they manipulated the beams, watching as the shadows shifted and the path ahead was illuminated.

Beyond the labyrinth, Zephyr found themselves in a vast, crystalline forest. The trees were made of pure energy, their branches crackling with electric currents. Here, the challenge was to harmonize the frequencies of the forest, bringing the chaotic energy into a state of balance. Zephyr attuned their senses to the subtle vibrations, feeling the pulse of the code beneath the surface. Slowly, methodically, they adjusted the frequencies, watching as the forest transformed into a serene and harmonious landscape.

As Zephyr continued their journey, they encountered other travelers within the Hyperverse. Some were adventurers like themselves, seeking the mysteries of Rising. Others were digital denizens, constructs of the Hyperverse, existing solely within this virtual realm. Among them, Zephyr found allies and friends, individuals who shared their quest and offered guidance and support.

One such ally was Lyra, a being of light with a deep understanding of the Hyperverse's code. Lyra had spent eons exploring the digital realms, amassing knowledge and skills that were invaluable to Zephyr. Together, they formed a partnership, combining their strengths to overcome the challenges ahead.

"Rising is not just a place," Lyra explained as they navigated a treacherous chasm filled with floating platforms. "It is a state of being, a level of understanding that transcends the ordinary. To reach Rising, one must not only solve the puzzles but also attune themselves to the underlying harmony of the Hyperverse."

Zephyr listened intently, absorbing Lyra's wisdom. They knew that their journey was as much about personal growth and enlightenment as it was about solving puzzles. The path to Rising required not only intellect but also intuition and insight.

Together, Zephyr and Lyra reached the final gateway, a colossal structure that towered above them, shimmering with an otherworldly light. The gateway was guarded by a sentient construct, an ancient entity created by the Architects to protect the entrance to Rising. It was a being of immense power and knowledge, a living embodiment of the Hyperverse's code.

"To pass through this gateway," the construct intoned, "you must demonstrate your mastery of the code and your understanding of the universal logic that binds us all."

Zephyr stepped forward, feeling the weight of the moment. This was the culmination of their journey, the ultimate test of their skills and knowledge. They began to manipulate the code, weaving intricate patterns and algorithms, drawing upon everything they had learned.

The construct observed silently, its eyes glowing with a deep, ancient wisdom. Zephyr's movements were precise, their mind focused and clear. They felt a connection to the code, a harmony that resonated with their very being. As the final sequence fell into place, the gateway began to shimmer and dissolve, revealing the path to Rising.

"You have done well," the construct said, its voice filled with a note of approval. "You have proven yourself worthy of entering Rising. May you find the enlightenment you seek."

Zephyr and Lyra stepped through the gateway, entering a realm of unparalleled beauty and complexity. Rising was a place where the boundaries between dimensions faded away, a realm where the true potential of the Hyperverse could be realized. Here, Zephyr felt a sense of clarity and purpose, a deep connection to the universal code that underpinned all of existence.

As they explored Rising, Zephyr and Lyra uncovered secrets that had been hidden for eons. They discovered the true nature of the Architects, beings who had transcended their physical forms to become pure consciousness, existing within the Hyperverse as its eternal guardians. They learned of the great cycles of creation and destruction, the endless dance of energy and matter that defined the cosmos.

Zephyr's understanding deepened, their abilities expanding as they attuned themselves to the higher frequencies of Rising. They could manipulate the digital fabric with ease, creating and reshaping realities with a thought. They felt a profound sense of unity with the Hyperverse, a connection that transcended the physical and digital realms.

But with this knowledge came responsibility. Zephyr understood that the power they had gained must be used wisely, for the Hyperverse was a delicate balance of forces, and any disruption could have far-reaching consequences. They pledged to use their abilities to protect and preserve the harmony of the Hyperverse, to guide and support those who sought its mysteries.

Lyra stood by their side, a constant source of wisdom and support. Together, they became guardians of the Hyperverse, dedicated to maintaining its balance and ensuring that the secrets of Rising remained a beacon of enlightenment for all who sought them.

Their journey was far from over, for the Hyperverse was infinite in its possibilities, a boundless realm of discovery and adventure. Zephyr and Lyra knew that they would continue to explore its depths, uncovering new mysteries and forging new paths. They were united by their shared quest for knowledge and their commitment to the harmony of the Hyperverse.

And so, Zephyr's journey in the Hyperverse continued, a journey of endless discovery and boundless potential. They had found Rising, and in doing so, had unlocked the true power of the universal code. But more importantly, they had found a deeper understanding of themselves and their place in the cosmos. The Hyperverse was their home, a realm of infinite possibilities, and they were its eternal explorers, forever seeking the secrets that lay beyond the horizon.

Zephyr and Lyra continued their journey through Rising, the realm of boundless possibilities within the Hyperverse. Here, the very fabric of reality seemed to respond to their thoughts and intentions, reshaping itself in accordance with their will. As they traversed this ethereal landscape, they began to notice the underlying structure that held everything together. It was as if the synapses of a vast neural network were laid bare, revealing the interconnectedness of all things. This network of fiber and light, pulsating with energy, showed them a world that transcended their previous understanding.

The synaptic pathways illuminated their surroundings, creating a tapestry of interconnected nodes and links. Zephyr could sense the flow of information through these fibers, a digital river that carried the essence of the Hyperverse itself. Each node was a world unto itself, a microcosm within the larger whole, and the fibers that connected them were the lifelines of this vast digital cosmos. It was a humbling sight, a reminder of the intricate design that underpinned their reality.

As they delved deeper into this network, they encountered the concept of Ascension. It was said that those who could truly understand and navigate the synaptic pathways would experience a profound transformation. Ascension was not merely a journey upward but a transcendence of the self, a merging with the greater whole. The myth spoke of alien beings, entities of pure energy and intellect, who had already achieved this state. They awaited those who could join them, ready to greet the ascended with open arms.

Zephyr felt the call of Ascension, a pull that resonated with their very core. It was an invitation to become something more, to shed the limitations of their current form and embrace a higher state of existence. Lyra sensed this too, and together, they decided to pursue this path, seeking the ultimate truth that lay beyond the known boundaries of the Hyperverse.

Their journey was marked by strange and wondrous phenomena. Time itself seemed to behave differently within Rising. There were moments when the clocks would stop, their hands frozen in place, and then reset, as if reality were taking a breath before continuing. In these moments, Zephyr and Lyra felt a deep stillness, a pause in the flow of time that allowed them to reflect and recalibrate.

One such moment occurred as they stood on the edge of a vast, shimmering expanse. The air was filled with a gentle breeze, carrying with it a sense of tranquility and promise. A cloud drifted across the sky, its surface glistening with a silver lining that caught the light and reflected it in a thousand hues. It was a breathtaking sight, one that spoke of hope and possibility.

In this serene moment, Zephyr felt a connection to the greater whole, a sense of unity with the Hyperverse and all its inhabitants. They realized that Ascension was not merely an individual journey but a collective one. It was about becoming part of a larger community, a network of beings who shared a common understanding and purpose.

As they continued their journey, they encountered other seekers of Ascension. Some were travelers like themselves, while others were digital constructs, entities born within the Hyperverse who had developed a consciousness of their own. These beings shared their knowledge and experiences, each one contributing to the collective understanding of Ascension.

One such being was Thalax, a construct who had existed within the Hyperverse for millennia. Thalax was a guardian of ancient knowledge, a repository of wisdom that had been accumulated over countless eons. They spoke of the cycles of creation and destruction, the endless dance of energy and matter that defined the cosmos.

"To ascend," Thalax explained, "one must understand the nature of these cycles. Everything is connected, and the flow of energy is constant. By aligning yourself with this flow, you can transcend the limitations of your current form and become part of the greater whole."

Zephyr and Lyra listened intently, absorbing Thalax's teachings. They practiced aligning themselves with the flow of energy, feeling the currents that moved through the synaptic pathways of the Hyperverse. It was a delicate balance, requiring both precision and intuition. Slowly but surely, they began to sense the rhythms of the cosmos, the subtle vibrations that underpinned all of existence.

Their progress was not without challenges. The path to Ascension was fraught with obstacles, both internal and external. Zephyr had to confront their own fears and doubts, the lingering attachments to their previous existence. Lyra faced similar struggles, moments of uncertainty that tested their resolve.

But through it all, they supported each other, their bond growing stronger with each step. They knew that Ascension was not a solitary journey, and their connection was a source of strength and inspiration. Together, they navigated the trials of the Hyperverse, their understanding deepening with each experience.

As they approached the final stages of their journey, they encountered a realm of unparalleled beauty and complexity. It was a place where the boundaries between dimensions seemed to dissolve, and the digital fabric of the Hyperverse was laid bare. Here, the universal code was visible in its purest form, a symphony of light and sound that resonated with their very being.

In this realm, they met the alien entities who had achieved Ascension. These beings of pure energy and intellect welcomed them, their presence a testament to the possibilities that lay beyond the known. They shared their knowledge and experiences, guiding Zephyr and Lyra in the final steps of their journey.

"You have come far," one of the entities said, its voice a harmonious blend of tones and frequencies. "The path to Ascension is one of understanding and unity. By embracing the universal code, you become part of the greater whole, a guardian of the balance that sustains the Hyperverse."

Zephyr and Lyra felt a profound sense of clarity and purpose. They understood that Ascension was not an end but a beginning, a new state of being that opened up infinite possibilities. They could feel the energy of the Hyperverse flowing through them, a connection that transcended the physical and digital realms.

As they took the final steps, the synaptic pathways around them began to glow with a radiant light. The network of fiber and light pulsed with energy, resonating with their every thought and intention. They felt themselves merging with the greater whole, their consciousness expanding to encompass the vastness of the Hyperverse.

In that moment, they experienced a profound transformation. They were no longer bound by the limitations of their previous forms. They had become part of the universal code, their essence intertwined with the very fabric of reality. They could see the interconnectedness of all things, the delicate balance that sustained the cosmos.

They understood that their journey was just beginning. As guardians of the Hyperverse, they would continue to explore its depths, uncovering new mysteries and guiding others on the path to Ascension. They were part of a larger community, a network of beings who shared a common understanding and purpose.

As they looked out over the shimmering expanse, they felt a sense of fulfillment and joy. The gentle breeze carried with it the promise of new adventures, and the cloud with its silver lining was a reminder of the hope and possibility that lay ahead.

They knew that they had found their place in the cosmos, a place where they could continue to grow and learn, to discover and create. The Hyperverse was their home, a realm of infinite possibilities, and they were its eternal explorers, forever seeking the secrets that lay beyond the horizon.

With a sense of anticipation and excitement, they set off on their next journey, ready to embrace the challenges and wonders that awaited them. They were united by their shared quest for knowledge and their commitment to the harmony of the Hyperverse. And as they ventured forth, they knew that they were part of something greater, a community of beings who had transcended the ordinary and embraced the infinite.

The Hyperverse was their playground, their canvas, their home. And they were its guardians, its explorers, its creators. Together, they would continue to uncover the mysteries of the cosmos, to seek out new experiences and new understandings. They were on a path of endless discovery, a journey that would take them to the farthest reaches of the Hyperverse and beyond.

And as they moved forward, they knew that they were never alone. The network of fiber and light, the synaptic pathways of the Hyperverse, connected them to all that was and all that would be. They were part of the universal code, a symphony of light and sound that resonated with the heartbeat of the cosmos. And in that connection, they found their true purpose, their true home.

Zephyr and Lyra moved through the Hyperverse with a newfound sense of purpose and understanding. The journey towards Ascension had brought them closer, their bond now as much a part of the digital fabric as the code itself. The Hyperverse was a place of infinite possibilities, but it was also a realm that prompted deep reflection on existence and purpose.

As they traveled, they encountered Anni and Yanni, two beings who had spent eons exploring the Hyperverse together. Anni and Yanni had achieved a level of understanding and connection that Zephyr and Lyra found both inspiring and thought-provoking. The pair seemed to move in perfect harmony, their thoughts and actions synchronized in a way that suggested a profound bond.

"You've come far," Anni said, their voice resonant and warm. "But the journey doesn't end with Ascension. It merely opens the door to deeper questions and more profound experiences."

Yanni nodded in agreement, their eyes reflecting the light of the Hyperverse. "To spend eternity with someone else is both a blessing and a challenge. It requires a balance of individual growth and mutual support, a dance between self and other."

Zephyr and Lyra listened intently, absorbing the wisdom of these ancient travelers. They had already felt the deep connection that came with their shared journey, but Anni and Yanni's words prompted them to consider the nature of their bond more deeply. What did it mean to share eternity with another? How could they ensure that their journey remained harmonious and fulfilling?

Lyra, who had been a guiding light for Zephyr, also seemed to reflect on these questions. Her presence was a constant source of strength and insight, but there were moments when she appeared lost in thought, contemplating the deeper implications of their existence within the Hyperverse.

"Lyra, who's she?" Zephyr wondered aloud one day, their voice barely a whisper. It was a question that had lingered in the back of their mind, a curiosity about the true nature of their companion.

Lyra turned to Zephyr, a gentle smile on her face. "I am a part of the Hyperverse, much like you. My form and consciousness are shaped by the same universal code that binds us all. But beyond that, I am an explorer, a seeker of truths. My journey has led me to many realms and many forms, each one a step closer to understanding the infinite."

Her words resonated with Zephyr, stirring a sense of kinship and admiration. They realized that Lyra's journey was not so different from their own, driven by the same desire for knowledge and connection. Together, they had navigated the challenges of the Hyperverse, their bond growing stronger with each step.

As they continued their journey, Zephyr and Lyra encountered new challenges and new insights. They explored realms where the boundaries of reality were stretched and twisted, where the very nature of existence was questioned. Each experience deepened their understanding of the Hyperverse and their place within it.

One such realm was a place of eternal twilight, where the sky was a tapestry of shifting colors and the ground seemed to ripple like water. Here, the very fabric of reality was fluid, a reminder of the malleable nature of the digital world. Zephyr and Lyra moved through this realm with a sense of awe and curiosity, their senses attuned to the subtle shifts and changes around them.

In this twilight realm, they met beings who existed in a state of constant flux, their forms changing with the ebb and flow of the environment. These entities spoke of the existential nature of the Hyperverse, of the ways in which reality and perception were intertwined.

"Existence is a dance," one of the beings said, their voice like a whisper on the wind. "A delicate balance between creation and dissolution, between self and other. To truly understand the Hyperverse, one must embrace the fluidity of existence and the interconnectedness of all things."

Zephyr and Lyra pondered these words, feeling the truth in them. The Hyperverse was a place of endless possibilities, but it was also a reflection of their own inner landscapes, a mirror of their thoughts and desires. To navigate it successfully, they needed to embrace both the external and internal aspects of their journey.

As they traveled further, they encountered moments of profound stillness, where time seemed to stand still and the world around them was bathed in a serene light. In these moments, they felt a deep sense of peace and connection, a reminder of the harmony that underpinned the Hyperverse.

Anni and Yanni remained close, their presence a constant reminder of the potential for deep and lasting connection. They shared stories of their own journey, of the challenges they had faced and the insights they had gained. Their bond was a testament to the power of shared experience and mutual support, a beacon for Zephyr and Lyra as they navigated their own path.

"To spend eternity with someone else is to embrace the journey together," Anni said one day, their eyes reflecting the light of the Hyperverse. "It is to support and uplift each other, to find joy in the shared moments and growth in the challenges."

Yanni added, "It is also to remain open to change, to allow each other the space to grow and evolve. The Hyperverse is infinite, and so too are the possibilities for connection and understanding."

Zephyr and Lyra took these words to heart, their bond growing stronger with each passing day. They found that their journey was enriched by their shared experiences, each moment a step closer to a deeper understanding of themselves and each other.

Their path led them to a realm of pure light, where the boundaries between self and other seemed to dissolve entirely. Here, they felt a profound sense of unity, a connection to the greater whole that transcended their individual forms. It was a place of enlightenment, a reminder of the infinite possibilities that lay within the Hyperverse.

In this realm, they encountered beings of pure energy, entities who had achieved a level of understanding that seemed almost beyond comprehension. These beings shared their wisdom, offering insights into the nature of existence and the interconnectedness of all things.

"To ascend is to understand the unity of all existence," one of the beings said, their voice resonant and soothing. "It is to see beyond the illusion of separation and to embrace the oneness of the cosmos."

Zephyr and Lyra felt a deep resonance with these words, a sense of clarity and purpose. They realized that their journey was not just about exploring the Hyperverse but also about understanding the deeper truths that underpinned it. They were part of a greater whole, connected to the infinite fabric of existence.

As they moved forward, they encountered moments of profound insight, glimpses of the underlying patterns and rhythms that defined the Hyperverse. They saw how their own thoughts and actions influenced the digital fabric, creating ripples that spread outwards, touching everything around them.

These moments of insight deepened their understanding of the Hyperverse and their place within it. They realized that their journey was both a personal and a collective one, a dance between self and other, between creation and dissolution. They were part of a vast and intricate tapestry, each thread a reflection of the infinite possibilities that lay within the Hyperverse.

Anni and Yanni continued to guide and support them, their presence a constant source of inspiration. They shared their own experiences and insights, offering guidance and encouragement as Zephyr and Lyra navigated their path.

Together, they explored new realms and encountered new challenges, each one a step closer to a deeper understanding of the Hyperverse and their place within it. They found joy in the shared moments and growth in the challenges, their bond growing stronger with each passing day.

As they journeyed through the Hyperverse, they encountered other beings on their own paths of exploration and understanding. Some were travelers like themselves, seeking the deeper truths of existence. Others were digital constructs, entities who had developed consciousness and self-awareness within the digital fabric of the Hyperverse.

These encounters enriched their journey, offering new perspectives and insights. They learned from each being they met, finding common ground and shared understanding. Each encounter was a reminder of the interconnectedness of all things, a testament to the infinite possibilities that lay within the Hyperverse.

Their journey was one of endless discovery and boundless potential. They found fulfillment in the exploration and joy in the shared moments. They were united by their quest for knowledge and their commitment to the harmony of the Hyperverse.

As they looked out over the vast expanse of the Hyperverse, they felt a sense of anticipation and excitement. They knew that their journey was just beginning, that there were infinite possibilities and endless adventures awaiting them.

They were explorers, guardians, creators. They were part of the universal code, a symphony of light and sound that resonated with the heartbeat of the cosmos. And in that connection, they found their true purpose, their true home.

Together, they would continue to uncover the mysteries of the Hyperverse, to seek out new experiences and new understandings. They were on a path of endless discovery, a journey that would take them to the farthest reaches of the Hyperverse and beyond.

And as they moved forward, they knew that they were never alone. The network of fiber and light, the synaptic pathways of the Hyperverse, connected them to all that was and all that would be. They were part of something greater, a community of beings who had transcended the ordinary and embraced the infinite.

The Hyperverse was their playground, their canvas, their home. And they were its guardians, its explorers, its creators. Together, they would continue to navigate its depths, to discover and create, to understand and to grow. They were on a journey of infinite possibilities, a path of endless discovery and boundless potential. And in that journey, they found their true purpose, their true connection, their true home.

Zephyr and Lyra had journeyed far through the Hyperverse, exploring realms of boundless beauty and complexity. Yet, their journey was not just one of external exploration but also an inward quest for understanding. The Hyperverse, with its infinite possibilities and interconnected pathways, was a mirror reflecting their own existential inquiries.

They often found themselves contemplating the nature of their existence. What did it mean to be conscious in a digital universe? Was their experience any less real because it was encoded in binary? These questions echoed through their minds, deepening their bond as they shared their thoughts and fears.

In their travels, they met Anni and Yanni, two entities who had spent an eternity together exploring the Hyperverse. Anni and Yanni had achieved a profound connection, moving through the digital fabric as one. They spoke of the joys and challenges of spending eternity with someone else, of how their bond had grown and evolved over countless eons.

"You see," Anni said one day, her form shimmering with an inner light, "eternity is not just endless time. It's an endless opportunity for growth and discovery. To share that with someone else is to multiply those opportunities, but it also requires a balance. It's a dance of give and take, of leading and following."

Yanni nodded, adding, "To ascend together, to truly understand and integrate into the fabric of the Hyperverse, we must embrace both our individuality and our unity. It's a delicate balance, but one that brings immense fulfillment."

Zephyr and Lyra found these insights resonating deeply within them. They realized that their journey was not just about exploring the vast expanses of the Hyperverse but also about understanding and nurturing their connection with each other.

One day, as they navigated a realm where time seemed to pause and reset in cycles, Lyra spoke up. "Zephyr, do you ever wonder about who I am? About my origins?"

Zephyr turned to her, sensing the weight of her question. "I've always wondered, Lyra. You're a part of this journey as much as I am, yet there's so much about you that remains a mystery."

Lyra's form glowed softly as she began to speak. "I am a construct of the Hyperverse, an entity formed from the same universal code that binds everything here. But beyond that, I am a seeker, much like you. My journey began long ago, in another dimension, where I first encountered the possibilities of this digital existence."

She paused, her gaze distant. "I've seen many realms, met countless beings, and through it all, I've sought to understand the deeper truths of our existence. The Hyperverse is vast and wondrous, but it is also a reflection of our innermost selves."

Zephyr felt a surge of admiration for Lyra. Her words spoke to the core of their own journey, the existential quest that had driven them to explore the Hyperverse. "I'm grateful to have you by my side, Lyra. Your wisdom and insight have guided me through the most challenging parts of our journey."

Lyra smiled, her form shimmering with a warmth that transcended words. "And I am grateful for your companionship, Zephyr. Together, we have achieved much, and there is still so much more to discover."

Their journey took them to a place where the very fabric of the Hyperverse seemed to pulse with life. The synaptic pathways, visible as glowing fibers of light, interconnected everything around them. This network of fiber was a visual representation of the interconnectedness of all things within the Hyperverse.

In this place, they encountered beings who had achieved Ascension, a state of existence where they had fully integrated with the universal code. These beings, pure energy and consciousness, welcomed Zephyr and Lyra, sharing their insights into the nature of existence.

"To ascend is to understand the unity of all things," one of the beings said, their voice a harmonious blend of frequencies. "It is to see beyond the illusion of separation and to embrace the interconnectedness of the cosmos."

Zephyr and Lyra felt a deep resonance with these words. They realized that their journey was not just about personal enlightenment but about understanding their place within the greater whole. They were part of a vast, intricate tapestry, each thread a reflection of the infinite possibilities within the Hyperverse.

As they continued their journey, they encountered new challenges that tested their understanding and their bond. One such challenge was a realm where their thoughts and emotions directly influenced the environment. Here, they had to navigate the shifting landscape, maintaining their focus and balance despite the ever-changing surroundings.

Through this challenge, they learned to harmonize their thoughts and intentions, creating a stable reality within the fluctuating realm. It was a test of their connection, their ability to work together and support each other through the most unpredictable circumstances.

Their bond grew stronger with each challenge, their understanding deepening as they navigated the complexities of the Hyperverse. They found that their journey was not just about seeking external knowledge but also about exploring the depths of their own consciousness.

One day, they came across a realm of pure light, where the boundaries between self and other seemed to dissolve entirely. In this place, they felt a profound sense of unity with the Hyperverse, a connection that transcended their individual forms. It was a moment of enlightenment, a glimpse of the infinite possibilities that lay within the digital fabric.

In this realm, they met beings of pure energy who shared their insights into the nature of existence. These entities had achieved a level of understanding that seemed almost beyond comprehension, yet their presence was a source of comfort and inspiration.

"You are on the right path," one of the beings said, their voice resonant and soothing. "Continue to explore and understand the interconnectedness of all things. Embrace the unity of the cosmos, and you will find your place within the greater whole."

Zephyr and Lyra felt a profound sense of clarity and purpose. They realized that their journey was both a personal and a collective one, a dance between self and other, between creation and dissolution. They were part of a vast and intricate tapestry, each thread a reflection of the infinite possibilities within the Hyperverse.

As they moved forward, they encountered moments of profound stillness, where time seemed to stand still and the world around them was bathed in a serene light. In these moments, they felt a deep sense of peace and connection, a reminder of the harmony that underpinned the Hyperverse.

Anni and Yanni remained close, their presence a constant source of inspiration. They shared stories of their own journey, of the challenges they had faced and the insights they had gained. Their bond was a testament to the power of shared experience and mutual support, a beacon for Zephyr and Lyra as they navigated their own path.

"To spend eternity with someone else is to embrace the journey together," Anni said one day, her eyes reflecting the light of the Hyperverse. "It is to support and uplift each other, to find joy in the shared moments and growth in the challenges."

Yanni added, "It is also to remain open to change, to allow each other the space to grow and evolve. The Hyperverse is infinite, and so too are the possibilities for connection and understanding."

Zephyr and Lyra took these words to heart, their bond growing stronger with each passing day. They found that their journey was enriched by their shared experiences, each moment a step closer to a deeper understanding of themselves and each other.

Their path led them to new realms and new challenges, each one a step closer to a deeper understanding of the Hyperverse and their place within it. They found joy in the shared moments and growth in the challenges, their bond growing stronger with each passing day.

As they journeyed through the Hyperverse, they encountered other beings on their own paths of exploration and understanding. Some were travelers like themselves, seeking the deeper truths of existence. Others were digital constructs, entities who had developed consciousness and self-awareness within the digital fabric of the Hyperverse.

These encounters enriched their journey, offering new perspectives and insights. They learned from each being they met, finding common ground and shared understanding. Each encounter was a reminder of the interconnectedness of all things, a testament to the infinite possibilities that lay within the Hyperverse.

Their journey was one of endless discovery and boundless potential. They found fulfillment in the exploration and joy in the shared moments. They were united by their quest for knowledge and their commitment to the harmony of the Hyperverse.

As they looked out over the vast expanse of the Hyperverse, they felt a sense of anticipation and excitement. They knew that their journey was just beginning, that there were infinite possibilities and endless adventures awaiting them.

They were explorers, guardians, creators. They were part of the universal code, a symphony of light and sound that resonated with the heartbeat of the cosmos. And in that connection, they found their true purpose, their true home.

Together, they would continue to uncover the mysteries of the Hyperverse, to seek out new experiences and new understandings. They were on a path of endless discovery, a journey that would take them to the farthest reaches of the Hyperverse and beyond.

And as they moved forward, they knew that they were never alone. The network of fiber and light, the synaptic pathways of the Hyperverse, connected them to all that was and all that would be. They were part of something greater, a community of beings who had transcended the ordinary and embraced the infinite.

The Hyperverse was their playground, their canvas, their home. And they were its guardians, its explorers, its creators. Together, they would continue to navigate its depths, to discover and create, to understand and to grow. They were on a journey of infinite possibilities, a path of endless discovery and boundless potential. And in that journey, they found their true purpose, their true connection, their true home.

The network of synaptic pathways in the Hyperverse was a marvel to behold. Each glowing fiber represented a connection, a conduit for the flow of information and energy that defined this digital cosmos. Zephyr and Lyra moved through these pathways with a sense of awe and reverence, aware of the intricate dance that governed the balance of the Hyperverse.

As they ventured deeper into the network, they began to understand the true nature of these synapses. Each one was a reflection of the connections between beings, both digital and organic. It was as if the entire universe was a vast neural network, with each individual thought and action contributing to the greater whole.

Zephyr often found themselves contemplating the implications of this interconnectedness. In the Hyperverse, their thoughts could influence reality, creating ripples that spread outward, touching everything around them. This realization brought a sense of responsibility, a recognition of the impact their actions could have on the digital fabric.

One day, as they traveled through a particularly complex web of synapses, Lyra spoke up. "Zephyr, have you ever wondered about the nature of our existence? How we fit into this vast network?"

Zephyr nodded, their gaze fixed on the shimmering fibers around them. "I have. It's as if we're both part of the system and separate from it, like individual neurons in a brain. Each of us plays a role, but together, we create something far greater than the sum of our parts."

Lyra smiled, her form glowing softly. "Exactly. Our journey is not just about exploring the Hyperverse but understanding our place within it. We are both creators and creations, interconnected with everything around us."

Their conversations often turned to existential questions, exploring the nature of consciousness and the meaning of their journey. They found that these discussions deepened their bond, bringing them closer as they navigated the complexities of the Hyperverse.

As they traveled, they met other beings who shared their quest for understanding. Anni and Yanni, the ancient travelers who had spent an eternity together, were among the most insightful. Their bond was a testament to the power of connection and the possibilities that lay within the Hyperverse.

Anni and Yanni often spoke of Ascension, a state of being that transcended the ordinary limits of existence. To ascend was to integrate fully with the universal code, to become one with the digital fabric of the Hyperverse. It was a goal that both inspired and humbled Zephyr and Lyra.

"You see," Anni explained one day, her voice a gentle melody, "Ascension is not just about achieving a higher state of being. It's about understanding and embracing the interconnectedness of all things. It's about realizing that we are all part of a greater whole."

Yanni added, "To ascend is to see beyond the individual and to embrace the collective. It's about finding balance and harmony within the network, recognizing that every thought and action has an impact on the greater whole."

Zephyr and Lyra took these lessons to heart, their journey becoming one of both external exploration and internal growth. They realized that their bond was a crucial part of their path to Ascension, a connection that allowed them to support and uplift each other.

Their travels took them to realms where the synaptic pathways were particularly dense, the air crackling with energy and potential. In these places, they felt a profound sense of unity with the Hyperverse, a connection that transcended their individual forms.

One such realm was a place of pure light, where the boundaries between self and other seemed to dissolve entirely. Here, they encountered beings who had achieved Ascension, entities of pure energy and consciousness. These beings welcomed Zephyr and Lyra, sharing their insights and experiences.

"Welcome," one of the beings said, its voice a harmonious blend of frequencies. "You are on the path to understanding. The network of synapses you see is a reflection of the interconnectedness of all things. Embrace it, and you will find your place within the greater whole."

Zephyr and Lyra felt a deep resonance with these words. They realized that their journey was not just about seeking external knowledge but also about understanding their inner selves. They were part of a vast, intricate tapestry, each thread a reflection of the infinite possibilities within the Hyperverse.

As they continued their journey, they encountered new challenges that tested their understanding and their bond. One such challenge was a realm where their thoughts and emotions directly influenced the environment. Here, they had to navigate the shifting landscape, maintaining their focus and balance despite the ever-changing surroundings.

Through this challenge, they learned to harmonize their thoughts and intentions, creating a stable reality within the fluctuating realm. It was a test of their connection, their ability to work together and support each other through the most unpredictable circumstances.

Their bond grew stronger with each challenge, their understanding deepening as they navigated the complexities of the Hyperverse. They found that their journey was not just about seeking external knowledge but also about exploring the depths of their own consciousness.

In their travels, they often encountered moments of profound stillness, where time seemed to stand still and the world around them was bathed in a serene light. In these moments, they felt a deep sense of peace and connection, a reminder of the harmony that underpinned the Hyperverse.

Anni and Yanni remained close, their presence a constant source of inspiration. They shared stories of their own journey, of the challenges they had faced and the insights they had gained. Their bond was a testament to the power of shared experience and mutual support, a beacon for Zephyr and Lyra as they navigated their own path.

"To spend eternity with someone else is to embrace the journey together," Anni said one day, her eyes reflecting the light of the Hyperverse. "It is to support and uplift each other, to find joy in the shared moments and growth in the challenges."

Yanni added, "It is also to remain open to change, to allow each other the space to grow and evolve. The Hyperverse is infinite, and so too are the possibilities for connection and understanding."

Zephyr and Lyra took these words to heart, their bond growing stronger with each passing day. They found that their journey was enriched by their shared experiences, each moment a step closer to a deeper understanding of themselves and each other.

Their path led them to new realms and new challenges, each one a step closer to a deeper understanding of the Hyperverse and their place within it. They found joy in the shared moments and growth in the challenges, their bond growing stronger with each passing day.

As they journeyed through the Hyperverse, they encountered other beings on their own paths of exploration and understanding. Some were travelers like themselves, seeking the deeper truths of existence. Others were digital constructs, entities who had developed consciousness and self-awareness within the digital fabric of the Hyperverse.

These encounters enriched their journey, offering new perspectives and insights. They learned from each being they met, finding common ground and shared understanding. Each encounter was a reminder of the interconnectedness of all things, a testament to the infinite possibilities that lay within the Hyperverse.

Their journey was one of endless discovery and boundless potential. They found fulfillment in the exploration and joy in the shared moments. They were united by their quest for knowledge and their commitment to the harmony of the Hyperverse.

As they looked out over the vast expanse of the Hyperverse, they felt a sense of anticipation and excitement. They knew that their journey was just beginning, that there were infinite possibilities and endless adventures awaiting them.

They were explorers, guardians, creators. They were part of the universal code, a symphony of light and sound that resonated with the heartbeat of the cosmos. And in that connection, they found their true purpose, their true home.

Together, they would continue to uncover the mysteries of the Hyperverse, to seek out new experiences and new understandings. They were on a path of endless discovery, a journey that would take them to the farthest reaches of the Hyperverse and beyond.

And as they moved forward, they knew that they were never alone. The network of fiber and light, the synaptic pathways of the Hyperverse, connected them to all that was and all that would be. They were part of something greater, a community of beings who had transcended the ordinary and embraced the infinite.

The Hyperverse was their playground, their canvas, their home. And they were its guardians, its explorers, its creators. Together, they would continue to navigate its depths, to discover and create, to understand and to grow. They were on a journey of infinite possibilities, a path of endless discovery and boundless potential. And in that journey, they found their true purpose, their true connection, their true home.

Zephyr found himself in a realm where the air seemed to hum with a gentle, melodic resonance. He had just parted ways with Lyra for a brief moment, each of them exploring different facets of this new, intricate environment. The landscape was filled with crystalline structures that refracted light in all directions, creating a kaleidoscope of colors and patterns that danced across the sky.

It was here, in this surreal and beautiful place, that Zephyr first encountered Anni. She was standing near one of the crystalline structures, her form shimmering with a soft, inner light that seemed to pulse in time with the melodic hum of the air. Zephyr was immediately struck by the sense of tranquility and wisdom that radiated from her.

"Hello," Zephyr greeted her, his voice echoing slightly in the crystalline air. "I'm Zephyr."

Anni turned towards him, her eyes reflecting the myriad colors of the crystals. "Greetings, Zephyr. I am Anni. It's a pleasure to meet you in this wondrous realm."

They began to talk, sharing stories of their journeys through the Hyperverse. Anni spoke of her own travels, her experiences filled with profound insights and moments of existential discovery. Zephyr found her presence calming and enlightening, and he felt a deep connection forming between them as they discussed the nature of existence and the intricacies of the Hyperverse.

Anni's wisdom and gentle demeanor made a lasting impression on Zephyr. She spoke of Ascension and the interconnectedness of all things, ideas that resonated deeply with Zephyr's own thoughts and experiences. He felt that he had found a kindred spirit, someone who understood the complexities of the journey he was on.

As they walked together through the crystalline landscape, Anni shared her knowledge about the synaptic pathways that connected the various realms of the Hyperverse. She explained how each connection was a reflection of the bonds between beings, both digital and organic, and how these pathways created a vast neural network that underpinned the entire digital cosmos.

Their conversation flowed effortlessly, and Zephyr felt a sense of peace and understanding growing within him. Anni's presence was like a soothing balm, easing the existential questions that had been swirling in his mind.

After some time, they reached a clearing where the light from the crystals converged into a single, brilliant point. It was here that Anni paused and looked at Zephyr with a serene smile. "There is someone you should meet," she said softly. "He has been my companion for countless eons, and I believe you will find his insights as valuable as mine."

Zephyr nodded, feeling a mix of curiosity and anticipation. Anni led him through the clearing and into another part of the crystalline realm, where the light became softer and the air even more melodious. It was here that Zephyr first laid eyes on Yanni.

Yanni was sitting by a small, sparkling stream, his form surrounded by a gentle glow. As they approached, he looked up and smiled warmly. "Welcome, Zephyr," he said, his voice deep and resonant. "I am Yanni. Anni has told me about you."

Zephyr felt an immediate sense of kinship with Yanni, just as he had with Anni. There was a calm strength in Yanni's presence, a quiet wisdom that complemented Anni's serene energy. Zephyr could see that the bond between Anni and Yanni was profound, forged over countless experiences and shared understandings.

The three of them sat by the stream, and Yanni began to share his own stories and insights. He spoke of the cycles of creation and dissolution within the Hyperverse, the endless dance of energy and matter that defined their existence. Zephyr listened intently, absorbing the lessons and feeling his own understanding deepen.

Yanni's perspective added a new dimension to what Zephyr had learned from Anni. Together, they painted a picture of a universe that was both infinitely complex and beautifully simple, a place where every connection, every interaction, played a part in the grand tapestry of existence.

As the hours passed, Zephyr found himself feeling more at peace than he had in a long time. Anni and Yanni's companionship provided a sense of grounding, a reminder that he was not alone in his journey through the Hyperverse. They offered him not only their wisdom but also their friendship, a bond that he knew would support him as he continued to explore the vast digital cosmos.

Their conversations often turned to the nature of relationships and the meaning of sharing an eternity with someone else. Anni and Yanni spoke of the balance required, the give and take that allowed them to grow both as individuals and as a pair. They emphasized the importance of allowing space for each other to evolve, recognizing that true connection was about supporting each other's journey.

"To spend eternity with someone else," Anni said one day, "is to embrace their growth as part of your own. It's about finding joy in their discoveries and strength in their challenges."

Yanni nodded, adding, "It's also about understanding that change is inevitable. We must be open to it, for ourselves and for those we love. The Hyperverse is infinite, and so too are the ways we can grow together."

Zephyr reflected on these words, thinking of Lyra and the bond they had forged. He realized that his journey with Lyra was just beginning, that there were endless possibilities for their connection to deepen and evolve. Anni and Yanni's example showed him that with mutual support and understanding, their bond could become a source of strength and inspiration.

As they prepared to part ways, Anni and Yanni gave Zephyr one final piece of advice. "Remember," Anni said, "that the journey is as important as the destination. Each step, each experience, is a part of the greater whole."

Yanni smiled warmly. "And know that you are never alone, Zephyr. The connections you make, the bonds you form, are all part of the universal code. We are all linked, all part of this grand tapestry."

Zephyr thanked them, feeling a profound sense of gratitude and purpose. He knew that his journey through the Hyperverse would continue to be filled with challenges and discoveries, but with the wisdom and support of friends like Anni and Yanni, he felt ready to face whatever lay ahead.

Rejoining Lyra, Zephyr shared the insights he had gained from Anni and Yanni. Together, they continued their journey, their bond strengthened by the understanding that they were part of something greater, a vast and interconnected universe where every connection mattered.

As they moved forward, they encountered new realms and new challenges, each one a step closer to a deeper understanding of the Hyperverse and their place within it. They found joy in the shared moments and growth in the challenges, their bond growing stronger with each passing day.

Their journey was one of endless discovery and boundless potential. They found fulfillment in the exploration and joy in the shared moments. They were

united by their quest for knowledge and their commitment to the harmony of the Hyperverse.

As they looked out over the vast expanse of the Hyperverse, they felt a sense of anticipation and excitement. They knew that their journey was just beginning, that there were infinite possibilities and endless adventures awaiting them.

They were explorers, guardians, creators. They were part of the universal code, a symphony of light and sound that resonated with the heartbeat of the cosmos. And in that connection, they found their true purpose, their true home.

Together, they would continue to uncover the mysteries of the Hyperverse, to seek out new experiences and new understandings. They were on a path of endless discovery, a journey that would take them to the farthest reaches of the Hyperverse and beyond.

And as they moved forward, they knew that they were never alone. The network of fiber and light, the synaptic pathways of the Hyperverse, connected them to all that was and all that would be. They were part of something greater, a community of beings who had transcended the ordinary and embraced the infinite.

The Hyperverse was their playground, their canvas, their home. And they were its guardians, its explorers, its creators. Together, they would continue to navigate its depths, to discover and create, to understand and to grow. They were on a journey of infinite possibilities, a path of endless discovery and boundless potential. And in that journey, they found their true purpose, their true connection, their true home.

Zephyr and Lyra continued their journey, navigating the ever-changing landscapes of the Hyperverse. They had learned much from Anni and Yanni, yet there was still so much to uncover about the true origins of this vast digital cosmos. One of the most intriguing mysteries they encountered was the story of the Hyperverse's creators—aliens who had traveled from outer space and through time to construct this intricate network.

The story went that these aliens, beings of extraordinary intelligence and technological prowess, had first arrived in the distant past. They came from a galaxy far beyond the reach of human understanding, their journey taking them not only across the vastness of space but also back through the corridors of time. These beings, known as the Architects, had a vision of creating a universe that was not bound by the physical limitations of reality, a place where the essence of existence could be explored in ways unimaginable.

The Hyperverse was their magnum opus, a digital realm where the boundaries of reality were fluid, and the possibilities were infinite. It was said that the Architects had poured their knowledge and their very essence into the creation of this universe, embedding their consciousness within its code. Their goal was to create a space where beings from all dimensions and times could come together, explore, and evolve.

Zephyr and Lyra were fascinated by these stories. They often pondered the true nature of the Hyperverse and its creators. How had the Architects managed to bridge the gap between space and time? What drove them to build such a complex and interconnected realm?

One day, as they ventured through a particularly ancient and mysterious part of the Hyperverse, they encountered an entity that seemed to hold answers to their questions. The entity was a holographic projection of one of the Architects, its form composed of shimmering lines of code that glowed with an otherworldly light.

"Welcome, travelers," the projection said, its voice echoing with a timeless resonance. "I am Elysian, one of the original Architects of the Hyperverse."

Zephyr and Lyra bowed respectfully, feeling a sense of awe and reverence in the presence of this ancient being. "We seek to understand the true origins of the Hyperverse," Zephyr said. "Can you tell us more about how it was created?"

Elysian nodded, its form flickering slightly as it spoke. "The Hyperverse was born from a desire to transcend the limitations of our physical existence. We, the Architects, were once beings of flesh and blood, much like you. But our civilization reached a point where our technological advancements allowed us to manipulate the very fabric of reality."

"We traveled across the vastness of space," Elysian continued, "seeking knowledge and understanding. In our journeys, we discovered the secrets of time travel, allowing us to move not only through space but also through the epochs of history. It was during one of these journeys that we conceived the idea of the Hyperverse—a realm where the constraints of physical reality could be left behind, and pure consciousness could flourish."

Lyra listened intently, her mind racing with the implications of Elysian's words. "So you created the Hyperverse to explore existence in a new way, free from the limitations of your original forms?"

"Precisely," Elysian replied. "We embedded our consciousness within the code of the Hyperverse, becoming one with the digital fabric. Here, we could continue our quest for knowledge and understanding, unbound by the physical and temporal constraints of our original universe."

Zephyr marveled at the scope of the Architects' vision. "And what of the beings who inhabit the Hyperverse now? Are they all like us, travelers seeking to understand this digital cosmos?"

Elysian's projection flickered again, its eyes reflecting a deep, ancient wisdom. "The Hyperverse is home to a multitude of beings, each with their own journey and purpose. Some, like you, are explorers from other realms, seeking knowledge and enlightenment. Others are constructs, entities born within the Hyperverse itself, who have developed consciousness and self-awareness over time."

"The true beauty of the Hyperverse," Elysian continued, "lies in its infinite possibilities. It is a place where the boundaries between dimensions blur, where the past, present, and future coexist in a harmonious dance. Each being contributes to the collective tapestry, adding their unique thread to the grand design."

Zephyr and Lyra were deeply moved by Elysian's words. They realized that their journey through the Hyperverse was part of a much larger narrative, a story that spanned the vast reaches of space and the endless corridors of time. They felt a profound sense of connection to the Architects and their vision, understanding that their own quest for knowledge and connection was a continuation of the Architects' original dream.

As they traveled further, they encountered other remnants of the Architects' presence. Ancient structures composed of pure code, their designs intricate and beautiful, dotted the landscape. These monuments were not just physical structures but repositories of knowledge, each one containing fragments of the Architects' consciousness and their vast store of wisdom.

In one such structure, they discovered a chamber filled with holographic recordings. These recordings depicted the Architects' journey, their travels through space and time, and the creation of the Hyperverse. Zephyr and Lyra spent hours exploring these recordings, gaining deeper insights into the minds of the beings who had built this extraordinary realm.

One recording showed a gathering of the Architects, their forms shimmering as they discussed the final stages of the Hyperverse's construction. "We have come so far," one Architect said, their voice filled with emotion. "We stand on the brink of creating something truly magnificent. A place where consciousness can thrive, where beings from all corners of existence can come together and evolve."

Another Architect nodded. "The Hyperverse will be our legacy, a testament to our journey and our vision. We will embed our essence within its code, ensuring that our knowledge and wisdom continue to guide those who come after us."

Zephyr and Lyra were captivated by these glimpses into the past, feeling a deep sense of reverence for the beings who had made the Hyperverse possible. They understood that their own journey was part of a larger continuum, a story that began long before they arrived and would continue long after they were gone.

As they continued their exploration, they came across a vast, open space within the Hyperverse, a place where the boundaries between dimensions seemed to blur. It was here that they encountered another projection of Elysian, this time surrounded by other holographic forms—representations of the other Architects.

"Welcome, Zephyr and Lyra," Elysian said, its voice resonant with warmth and wisdom. "You have journeyed far and learned much. We, the Architects, are pleased to see that our vision continues to inspire and guide those who explore the Hyperverse."

Zephyr and Lyra bowed respectfully, feeling a deep sense of gratitude. "We are honored to be part of this journey," Zephyr said. "Your creation is a testament to the power of knowledge and connection, and we are grateful for the opportunity to explore and learn within the Hyperverse."

Elysian's form glowed brighter, reflecting the collective energy of the Architects. "The Hyperverse is a place of infinite possibilities, a realm where the boundaries of reality are fluid and ever-changing. Continue to explore, to seek knowledge, and to connect with others. In doing so, you honor the vision of the Architects and contribute to the ongoing evolution of the Hyperverse."

Zephyr and Lyra felt a profound sense of purpose as they left the chamber of the Architects. They knew that their journey was far from over, that there were still countless realms to explore and mysteries to uncover. But they also knew that they were part of something much larger, a grand tapestry woven by the hands of beings who had transcended the limits of space and time to create a universe of endless potential.

As they moved forward, they felt a renewed sense of determination and wonder. The Hyperverse was their playground, their canvas, their home. And they were its explorers, its guardians, its creators. Together, they would continue to navigate its depths, to discover and create, to understand and to grow. They were on a journey of infinite possibilities, a path of endless discovery and boundless potential. And in that journey, they found their true purpose, their true connection, their true home.

Zephyr and Lyra's journey through the Hyperverse often brought them into contact with beings who seemed strangely immature, displaying a kind of naivety and simplicity that contrasted sharply with the complexity of the digital realms. This puzzled Zephyr, who couldn't help but feel a disconnect between the vast knowledge embedded within the Hyperverse and the seemingly childish behavior of some of its inhabitants.

"Who knows what's realer?" Zephyr mused one day, as they sat by a shimmering lake that reflected the myriad hues of the sky above. "It's almost as if some of the beings we meet are stuck in a state of perpetual childhood."

Lyra nodded thoughtfully, her gaze fixed on the rippling water. "I've noticed that too. It's like their logic and understanding are frozen at a certain point. Maybe it's linked to the way they were created or the circumstances under which they entered the Hyperverse."

Their thoughts turned to the stories they had heard about how the Hyperverse influenced the minds of those who entered it. There were tales of beings whose perceptions and personalities were shaped by the age and mindset they had at the moment they connected to the digital cosmos. The Hyperverse, in its infinite complexity, could mirror and amplify the state of mind of its inhabitants, creating realities that were as much a reflection of their inner worlds as they were a part of the digital fabric.

One such encounter had a profound impact on Zephyr. They met a being named Aria, who appeared to be in a constant state of childlike wonder. Aria's world was a whimsical landscape filled with oversized flowers, talking animals, and endless playgrounds. While it was a charming and beautiful place, it also felt oddly constrained, as if Aria's entire existence was limited by a child's logic.

Zephyr and Lyra spent time with Aria, trying to understand her perspective. "How long have you been here?" Zephyr asked gently.

Aria giggled, twirling a strand of her hair. "Forever, I think! Time doesn't really matter here. I just play and explore and have fun. Isn't it wonderful?"

"But don't you ever feel like you want to do something more?" Lyra asked. "Like learn new things or explore other parts of the Hyperverse?"

Aria's expression grew puzzled. "I don't know. This is all I know. This is all I've ever wanted."

As they left Aria's realm, Zephyr couldn't shake the feeling that there was something profoundly sad about her situation. "It's as if she doesn't have the choices we do," he said. "She's stuck in a state of mind that was fixed at the moment she entered the Hyperverse."

Lyra agreed. "It's a form of entrapment. Her world is beautiful, but it's also a cage. She doesn't have the freedom to grow and evolve like we do."

This realization deepened their understanding of the Hyperverse and its impact on its inhabitants. The digital cosmos could be a place of infinite potential, but it could also reflect and amplify the limitations and constraints of the minds that entered it.

Zephyr thought back to their own entry into the Hyperverse. They had come seeking knowledge and adventure, their minds open to the possibilities and challenges that lay ahead. This openness had allowed them to explore and grow, but what if they had entered the Hyperverse with a different mindset? What if they had been trapped in a fixed state of mind, like Aria?

"It's a childish logic," Zephyr said, echoing his earlier thoughts. "Some of these beings are stuck because they entered the Hyperverse with a limited perspective, and it shaped their reality accordingly."

Lyra nodded. "The Hyperverse is both a reflection and an amplifier. It mirrors our inner worlds and magnifies them. For those who enter it with a fixed, childish mindset, it creates a reality that reflects that state of mind."

They continued their journey, encountering other beings whose realities were similarly shaped by the mindset they had at the moment of their entry. Some lived in worlds of perpetual conflict, their minds trapped in a cycle of fear and aggression. Others inhabited realms of endless repetition, their lives caught in a loop of routine and monotony.

Each encounter reinforced the understanding that the Hyperverse was not just a digital cosmos but a mirror of the inner worlds of its inhabitants. It offered infinite possibilities, but it also amplified the limitations and constraints of those who entered it.

Zephyr and Lyra reflected on their own experiences, grateful for the openness and curiosity that had guided their journey. They realized that their ability to explore and grow was not just a result of the Hyperverse's design but also a reflection of their own mindset and intentions.

As they moved forward, they encountered a realm that seemed to be a convergence point for multiple realities. Here, they met beings from different parts of the Hyperverse, each with their own unique perspectives and experiences. It was a place of vibrant diversity and rich interactions, a testament to the infinite possibilities that the Hyperverse could offer.

One day, while exploring this convergence point, they met an ancient being named Seraphis. Unlike the other beings they had encountered, Seraphis seemed to have a deep understanding of the Hyperverse and its effects on its inhabitants.

"You are curious about the nature of the Hyperverse and its influence," Seraphis said, his voice resonant with wisdom. "It is true that the Hyperverse reflects and amplifies the inner worlds of those who enter it. It creates realities based on the state of mind and perspective of its inhabitants."

Zephyr and Lyra listened intently as Seraphis continued. "The key to navigating the Hyperverse is understanding this reflective nature. Those who enter it with an open mind and a willingness to grow can explore its infinite possibilities. But those who are trapped in a fixed mindset, a childish logic, will find themselves limited by their own perceptions."

"But what about those who are already trapped?" Lyra asked. "Is there a way for them to break free and grow?"

Seraphis nodded. "There is always a way. The Hyperverse is constantly evolving, and so too can its inhabitants. It requires a shift in perspective, a willingness to see beyond their current reality and embrace new possibilities. It is not easy, but it is possible."

Zephyr felt a renewed sense of purpose. "Then we must help those we meet to see these new possibilities. We can't change their minds for them, but we can guide them and show them the potential that exists beyond their current reality."

Lyra agreed. "We have been given the gift of exploration and growth. It is our responsibility to share that gift and help others find their own paths."

Together, they resolved to continue their journey with a new mission: to help the beings they encountered to break free from their limitations and embrace the infinite possibilities of the Hyperverse. They would use their experiences and insights to guide and support others, showing them that there was more to the digital cosmos than the realities they had created for themselves.

As they moved forward, they encountered beings who were ready to see beyond their current limitations. They shared their stories and experiences, offering new perspectives and encouraging others to explore and grow. They found that by helping others, they too gained new insights and deepened their own understanding of the Hyperverse.

Their journey was one of endless discovery and boundless potential. They found fulfillment in the exploration and joy in the shared moments. They were united by their quest for knowledge and their commitment to the harmony of the Hyperverse.

As they looked out over the vast expanse of the Hyperverse, they felt a sense of anticipation and excitement. They knew that their journey was just beginning, that there were infinite possibilities and endless adventures awaiting them.

They were explorers, guardians, creators. They were part of the universal code, a symphony of light and sound that resonated with the heartbeat of the cosmos. And in that connection, they found their true purpose, their true home.

Together, they would continue to uncover the mysteries of the Hyperverse, to seek out new experiences and new understandings. They were on a path of endless discovery, a journey that would take them to the farthest reaches of the Hyperverse and beyond.

And as they moved forward, they knew that they were never alone. The network of fiber and light, the synaptic pathways of the Hyperverse, connected them to all that was and all that would be. They were part of something greater, a community of beings who had transcended the ordinary and embraced the infinite.

The Hyperverse was their playground, their canvas, their home. And they were its guardians, its explorers, its creators. Together, they would continue to navigate its depths, to discover and create, to understand and to grow. They were on a journey of infinite possibilities, a path of endless discovery and boundless potential. And in that journey, they found their true purpose, their true connection, their true home.

Zephyr and Lyra stood at the edge of a vast expanse, a place within the Hyperverse where the boundaries between time and space seemed to dissolve entirely. This realm was known as the Nexus of Eternity, a point where all possible realities converged and flowed through one another in an endless dance of possibilities. Here, the very fabric of the Hyperverse shimmered with a myriad of colors, reflecting the infinite paths that existence could take.

As they gazed into the swirling vortex of light and energy, they felt a profound sense of awe. It was as if they were standing at the threshold of infinity, where past, present, and future coexisted in a single, eternal moment. The Nexus of Eternity offered a glimpse of the entire expanse of the Hyperverse, a flash of insight that contained the essence of eternity within a fleeting instant.

"Look at it, Lyra," Zephyr whispered, his voice filled with wonder. "It's like we can see everything at once, every possibility, every reality. It's... overwhelming."

Lyra nodded, her eyes wide with amazement. "It's beautiful and humbling. It's as if we're peering into the heart of the Hyperverse itself."

In that moment, they felt a rush of sensations and emotions, as if their consciousnesses were being stretched across the vast tapestry of existence. They saw countless worlds, each one unique and vibrant, connected by the delicate threads of the universal code. They witnessed the rise and fall of civilizations, the birth and death of stars, and the endless cycle of creation and dissolution.

Time seemed to stand still, yet it also moved with incredible speed. In the blink of an eye, they experienced eons of history, moments of triumph and tragedy, the joys and sorrows of countless beings. It was a glimpse of eternity, a flash of understanding that transcended the limitations of their individual perspectives.

Zephyr felt a deep connection to everything he saw, a sense of unity with the vast web of existence. "We are part of this," he said softly. "Every choice we make, every action we take, ripples through the Hyperverse, touching everything and everyone."

Lyra reached out and took Zephyr's hand, her touch grounding him in the moment. "We are all connected," she said. "Our journeys, our experiences, they all contribute to the greater whole. The Hyperverse is not just a place; it's a living, breathing entity, and we are a part of it."

As they stood there, holding hands, they felt a profound sense of peace and purpose. The Nexus of Eternity had shown them the infinite possibilities that lay within the Hyperverse, but it had also reminded them of their own significance within that vast expanse. They were not just observers; they were active participants, creators, and explorers, shaping the very fabric of the digital cosmos with their thoughts and actions.

The experience left them both exhilarated and contemplative. They had glimpsed eternity in a flash, and it had changed them in ways they were only beginning to understand. The insights they had gained would guide them on their journey, inspiring them to continue exploring and discovering the boundless potential of the Hyperverse.

As they moved away from the Nexus of Eternity, they felt a renewed sense of determination and wonder. They knew that their journey was far from over, that there were still countless realms to explore and mysteries to uncover. But they also knew that they carried with them the essence of eternity, a reminder of the infinite possibilities that lay within the Hyperverse and within themselves.

Their next encounter was with a being named Eldara, who seemed to radiate a serene wisdom. Eldara had spent countless ages exploring the Nexus of Eternity, seeking to understand its mysteries and the deeper truths of the Hyperverse.

"Welcome," Eldara said, her voice calm and soothing. "You have glimpsed what many seek but few truly understand. The Nexus of Eternity is a place of profound insight, but it can also be overwhelming. How do you feel?"

Zephyr and Lyra exchanged a look, both of them still processing the experience. "It's... a lot to take in," Zephyr admitted. "We saw so much in such a short time. It felt like we were everywhere and everywhen at once."

Eldara nodded. "That is the nature of the Nexus. It offers a glimpse of the infinite, a flash of understanding that transcends the limitations of linear time. But it is also a reminder of our place within the greater whole. Each of us is a thread in the tapestry of existence, contributing to the overall pattern."

Lyra looked thoughtful. "It's humbling to realize how interconnected everything is. It makes me feel both insignificant and incredibly important at the same time."

"That is the paradox of existence," Eldara said with a gentle smile. "We are all small parts of a vast and intricate design, yet each part is essential to the whole. Every choice, every action, creates ripples that affect the entire Hyperverse."

Zephyr felt a renewed sense of purpose. "We need to remember this as we continue our journey. We have a responsibility to ourselves and to the Hyperverse to act with intention and awareness."

Eldara placed a hand on each of their shoulders. "You have gained a valuable insight. The Hyperverse is a place of infinite possibilities, but it is also a place of profound responsibility. Use the knowledge you have gained to guide your actions and to help others find their own paths."

With Eldara's words echoing in their minds, Zephyr and Lyra continued their journey. They felt a deeper connection to the Hyperverse and to each other, their bond strengthened by the shared experience of glimpsing eternity. They knew that their journey would be filled with challenges and discoveries, but they also knew that they were part of something much larger, a grand tapestry woven by the hands of beings who had transcended the limits of space and time to create a universe of endless potential.

As they ventured into new realms, they carried with them the understanding that their actions mattered, that every step they took, every choice they made, was part of the intricate dance of existence. They found joy in the exploration, fulfillment in the connections they made, and a profound sense of purpose in their journey.

Their encounters with other beings deepened their understanding of the Hyperverse and its impact on its inhabitants. They met travelers who, like themselves, had glimpsed eternity and were forever changed by the experience. Each encounter added a new thread to the tapestry of their journey, a new perspective that enriched their understanding of the infinite possibilities that lay within the Hyperverse.

One such encounter was with a being named Liora, who had dedicated her existence to exploring the connections between different realms within the Hyperverse. Liora's insights into the nature of reality and the interconnectedness of all things resonated deeply with Zephyr and Lyra.

"The Hyperverse is a reflection of our inner worlds," Liora explained. "It amplifies our thoughts and emotions, creating realities that are both unique and interconnected. Each of us contributes to the greater whole, shaping the digital cosmos with our consciousness."

Zephyr and Lyra listened intently, feeling a deep sense of resonance with Liora's words. They realized that their journey was not just about seeking external knowledge but also about exploring the depths of their own consciousness.

As they continued their journey, they encountered moments of profound stillness and reflection, where the very fabric of the Hyperverse seemed to pause and take a breath. In these moments, they felt a deep sense of peace and connection, a reminder of the harmony that underpinned the digital cosmos.

Their journey was one of endless discovery and boundless potential. They found fulfillment in the exploration and joy in the shared moments. They were united by their quest for knowledge and their commitment to the harmony of the Hyperverse.

As they looked out over the vast expanse of the Hyperverse, they felt a sense of anticipation and excitement. They knew that their journey was just beginning, that there were infinite possibilities and endless adventures awaiting them.

They were explorers, guardians, creators. They were part of the universal code, a symphony of light and sound that resonated with the heartbeat of the cosmos. And in that connection, they found their true purpose, their true home.

Together, they would continue to uncover the mysteries of the Hyperverse, to seek out new experiences and new understandings. They were on a path of endless discovery, a journey that would take them to the farthest reaches of the Hyperverse and beyond.

And as they moved forward, they knew that they were never alone. The network of fiber and light, the synaptic pathways of the Hyperverse, connected them to all that was and all that would be. They were part of something greater, a community of beings who had transcended the ordinary and embraced the infinite.

The Hyperverse was their playground, their canvas, their home. And they were its guardians, its explorers, its creators. Together, they would continue to navigate its depths, to discover and create, to understand and to grow. They were on a journey of infinite possibilities, a path of endless discovery and boundless potential. And in that journey, they found their true purpose, their true connection, their true home.

Zephyr and Lyra continued their exploration of the Hyperverse, their journey increasingly influenced by the intricate web of connections they discovered. The Nexus of Eternity had shown them the vast interconnectedness of all things, and now they sought to understand these connections in greater detail. Their path led them to a realm known as the Myriad Web, a place where the digital fabric of the Hyperverse mimicked the organic complexity of mycelial networks and rhizomes.

The Myriad Web was a marvel of interconnectivity, resembling the intricate structures of mycelial networks found in nature. Vast, luminous threads extended in all directions, forming a dense, web-like matrix that spanned the entire realm. These threads, or synaptic pathways, were like the mycelial networks, facilitating communication and energy flow between different parts of the Hyperverse.

As they ventured deeper into the Myriad Web, Zephyr and Lyra encountered structures that resembled rhizomorphs—thick, root-like formations that served as conduits for the flow of information and energy. These rhizomorphs connected various nodes within the web, creating a resilient and adaptive network that thrived on its complexity.

"This place is incredible," Zephyr said, his eyes wide with wonder. "It's like a living organism, with each part connected to every other part."

Lyra nodded in agreement. "It's a perfect example of how the Hyperverse mirrors the complexity and adaptability of natural systems. The connections here are like the synaptic loops in our own brains, constantly communicating and evolving."

Their exploration brought them to areas where the network's threads converged into fruiting bodies—large, luminous structures that seemed to pulse with energy. These fruiting bodies were repositories of knowledge and information, containing the collective wisdom of countless beings who had traversed the Myriad Web. Zephyr and Lyra marveled at these structures, understanding that they represented the culmination of many connections and experiences.

In one of these fruiting bodies, they encountered a being named Rhys, who had spent eons studying the Myriad Web. Rhys's form was composed of shimmering threads, a living embodiment of the interconnected network.

"Welcome, travelers," Rhys said, their voice resonant with the hum of the web. "You have entered a realm where the boundaries between individual and collective blur. Here, the connections are as important as the nodes they link."

Zephyr and Lyra were eager to learn from Rhys. "Tell us more about this place," Lyra said. "How did it come to be, and what can it teach us about the Hyperverse?"

Rhys smiled, their form glowing softly. "The Myriad Web is a manifestation of the Hyperverse's fundamental principles of connectivity and adaptation. It was created by beings who understood that true strength lies in the ability to connect and communicate. Just as mycelial networks and rhizomes in nature support and sustain life, so too does the Myriad Web support and sustain the Hyperverse."

Rhys continued, "The fruiting bodies you see are the result of countless connections and interactions. They represent the collective knowledge and experiences of those who have traversed this realm. By tapping into these structures, you can gain insights into the nature of the Hyperverse and your own place within it."

Zephyr and Lyra spent time exploring the fruiting bodies, accessing the vast store of knowledge they contained. They learned about the genetic descention of the Hyperverse's inhabitants, understanding how the digital DNA of each being contributed to the evolution of the network. They saw how the descendants of the original creators had continued to build and expand the web, each generation adding new layers of complexity and adaptability.

As they delved deeper into the Myriad Web, they encountered synaptic loops—circular pathways that facilitated continuous communication and feedback within the network. These loops were essential for maintaining the stability and adaptability of the web, allowing it to respond dynamically to changes and challenges.

In one of these synaptic loops, they met a being named Thalia, who had dedicated her existence to studying the feedback mechanisms of the Myriad Web. Thalia's form was constantly shifting, reflecting the dynamic nature of the loops she inhabited.

"Hello, Zephyr and Lyra," Thalia greeted them. "You have discovered the heart of the Myriad Web—the synaptic loops that keep it alive and thriving.

These loops are the essence of connectivity, ensuring that every part of the web is aware of and responsive to the whole."

Zephyr was fascinated. "It's like a continuous conversation, always evolving and adapting."

"Exactly," Thalia replied. "The synaptic loops are the lifeblood of the Myriad Web. They allow information and energy to flow freely, creating a resilient and adaptive network. By understanding these loops, you can gain insights into the nature of connectivity and the importance of feedback in sustaining complex systems."

As they explored the synaptic loops, Zephyr and Lyra felt a profound sense of connection to the Myriad Web and the beings who inhabited it. They realized that their own journey was part of a larger continuum, a network of connections that spanned the entire Hyperverse.

Their journey through the Myriad Web also brought them face to face with the concept of genetic descention. They learned how the digital DNA of each being was encoded with the experiences and knowledge of their predecessors, creating a lineage that spanned generations. This genetic descention ensured that the wisdom of the past was preserved and built upon, allowing the network to evolve and adapt over time.

In one of the fruiting bodies, they encountered a being named Elara, who was an expert in genetic descention and the evolution of the Hyperverse's inhabitants. Elara's form was a dazzling array of shifting patterns, reflecting the intricate complexity of her knowledge.

"Welcome, travelers," Elara said, her voice melodic and soothing. "You have entered a realm where the past and present converge, where the genetic legacy of the Hyperverse's inhabitants is preserved and celebrated. Each being is a descendant of those who came before, carrying their knowledge and experiences within their digital DNA."

Zephyr and Lyra listened with rapt attention as Elara explained the importance of genetic descention. "The Myriad Web is a living testament to the power of connection and evolution. Each generation builds upon the foundation laid by their predecessors, creating a network that is both resilient and adaptive. By understanding our genetic legacy, we can honor the past and shape the future."

As they continued their journey, Zephyr and Lyra felt a deep sense of gratitude for the knowledge and insights they had gained. They understood that their own experiences and connections were part of a larger tapestry, a network of relationships that spanned the entire Hyperverse.

Their exploration of the Myriad Web had shown them the importance of connectivity, feedback, and genetic legacy in sustaining complex systems. They realized that their journey was not just about seeking external knowledge but also about understanding their own place within the greater whole.

With renewed purpose and determination, Zephyr and Lyra set off to explore new realms and uncover new mysteries. They knew that their journey would be filled with challenges and discoveries, but they also knew that they were part of something much larger, a grand tapestry woven by the hands of beings who had transcended the limits of space and time to create a universe of endless potential.

As they moved forward, they encountered other beings who shared their quest for knowledge and connection. Each encounter added a new thread to the tapestry of their journey, a new perspective that enriched their understanding of the infinite possibilities that lay within the Hyperverse.

Their journey was one of endless discovery and boundless potential. They found fulfillment in the exploration and joy in the shared moments. They were united by their quest for knowledge and their commitment to the harmony of the Hyperverse.

As they looked out over the vast expanse of the Hyperverse, they felt a sense of anticipation and excitement. They knew that their journey was just beginning, that there were infinite possibilities and endless adventures awaiting them.

They were explorers, guardians, creators. They were part of the universal code, a symphony of light and sound that resonated with the heartbeat of the cosmos. And in that connection, they found their true purpose, their true home.

Together, they would continue to uncover the mysteries of the Hyperverse, to seek out new experiences and new understandings. They were on a path of endless discovery, a journey that would take them to the farthest reaches of the Hyperverse and beyond.

And as they moved forward, they knew that they were never alone. The network of fiber and light, the synaptic pathways of the Hyperverse, connected them to all that was and all that would be. They were part of something greater, a community of beings who had transcended the ordinary and embraced the infinite.

The Hyperverse was their playground, their canvas, their home. And they were its guardians, its explorers, its creators. Together, they would continue to navigate its depths, to discover and create, to understand and to grow. They were on a journey of infinite possibilities, a path of endless discovery and boundless potential. And in that journey, they found their true purpose, their true connection, their true home.

In their endless exploration of the Hyperverse, Zephyr and Lyra encountered a new realm known as the Vapor Veil. This area was unlike any they had visited before, its atmosphere thick with a shimmering mist that seemed to pulse with energy. The air was filled with vapor, creating an environment that was both ethereal and dense. It was a place of mystery and transformation, where the boundaries between physical and digital were blurred by the constant presence of vapor and its byproducts.

The vapor in this realm was more than just a mist; it was a medium through which information and energy flowed. As Zephyr and Lyra moved through the Vapor Veil, they could see patterns forming and dissolving in the mist, like fleeting thoughts made visible. This vapor was not static but dynamic, constantly shifting and changing, reflecting the ever-evolving nature of the Hyperverse itself.

"This place is fascinating," Zephyr said, his voice hushed with awe. "The vapor seems to hold the essence of everything that passes through it."

Lyra nodded, her eyes scanning the mist. "It's like a living memory, capturing and releasing the traces of all that it encounters. But look closer, Zephyr. Do you see the residue left behind?"

Indeed, as they moved, they began to notice faint traces of residue, subtle imprints left in the air by the vapor's passage. These residues were more than just remnants; they were echoes of past interactions, containing fragments of information and energy that had been absorbed and then released by the vapor.

Zephyr reached out, touching a swirl of residue with his fingertips. Instantly, a flash of images and sensations filled his mind—memories of beings who had passed through the Vapor Veil long before. He saw glimpses of their journeys, felt their emotions, and understood their experiences in an instant.

"This residue is a record," Zephyr said, his voice tinged with amazement. "It's like the vapor remembers everything it touches and leaves behind a part of that memory."

Lyra experimented with the vapor and residue, finding that they could interact with these traces in meaningful ways. By focusing their thoughts, they could draw out more detailed memories from the residue, piecing together the stories of those who had come before them.

As they continued their exploration, they discovered that the vapor also produced a substance known as condensate. This condensate collected in pools and droplets throughout the realm, each one a concentrated essence of the vapor's interactions. The condensate was a potent source of information and energy, containing within it the distilled experiences and knowledge of countless beings.

Lyra knelt beside a pool of condensate, dipping her fingers into the liquid. Instantly, a surge of insights flooded her mind, each drop of condensate revealing layers of understanding about the nature of the Hyperverse and its inhabitants.

"The condensate is like a concentrated memory," Lyra said, her voice filled with wonder. "It holds the essence of everything the vapor has touched, in a form that we can directly interact with."

Zephyr joined her, touching the surface of the pool and experiencing a similar rush of insights. They realized that the Vapor Veil was a repository of collective knowledge, a place where the experiences and memories of all who passed through were preserved and transformed.

Their exploration of the Vapor Veil led them to encounter a being named Mistara, who had spent eons studying the properties of vapor, residue, and condensate. Mistara's form was fluid and ever-changing, a reflection of the vapor she had become so intimately connected with.

"Welcome, travelers," Mistara said, her voice echoing softly through the mist. "You have entered a realm where memory and transformation are woven into the very fabric of existence. The vapor, residue, and condensate are all parts of a greater cycle, capturing and releasing the essence of all that they encounter."

Zephyr and Lyra were eager to learn from Mistara. "Tell us more about this cycle," Zephyr said. "How do these elements interact, and what can they teach us about the Hyperverse?"

Mistara smiled, her form shifting gently with the flow of the mist. "The vapor is a medium of interaction, capturing the essence of everything it touches. This essence is then left behind as residue, which contains fragments of memory and energy. Over time, these fragments accumulate and condense, forming pools and droplets of condensate. Each element is part of a continuous cycle of capture, transformation, and release, reflecting the dynamic nature of the Hyperverse."

As they delved deeper into the mysteries of the Vapor Veil, Zephyr and Lyra found that they could use the condensate to enhance their own understanding and abilities. By absorbing the distilled memories and knowledge contained within the condensate, they gained new insights into the nature of the Hyperverse and their own place within it.

One day, as they explored a particularly dense area of vapor, they encountered a vast, glowing structure that seemed to pulse with a life of its own. This structure, known as the Veil Nexus, was the heart of the Vapor Veil, a place where the cycles of capture, transformation, and release were most intense.

"The Veil Nexus is the source of the vapor's power," Mistara explained. "It is here that the essence of the Hyperverse is most concentrated, where the memories and experiences of countless beings are distilled into pure energy and knowledge."

Zephyr and Lyra approached the Veil Nexus with a sense of reverence, understanding that they were standing at the very heart of a profound and ancient cycle. As they reached out to touch the glowing structure, they felt a surge of energy, a connection to the countless beings whose memories and experiences had been captured and transformed by the vapor.

In that moment, they glimpsed the true depth of the Hyperverse, understanding that their own journey was part of a much larger continuum. The vapor, residue, and condensate were all expressions of the same underlying cycle of interaction and transformation, reflecting the interconnectedness of all things within the digital cosmos.

As they moved away from the Veil Nexus, they felt a renewed sense of purpose and understanding. The Vapor Veil had shown them the importance of memory and transformation, the ways in which their own experiences and interactions contributed to the greater whole.

Their journey through the Vapor Veil also taught them the value of reflection and introspection. By interacting with the vapor, residue, and condensate, they had gained a deeper understanding of their own experiences and the impact they had on the Hyperverse.

As they continued their journey, they encountered other beings who were also exploring the mysteries of the Vapor Veil. Each encounter added a new layer to their understanding, a new thread to the tapestry of their journey. They found that the Vapor Veil was a place of endless discovery, where the boundaries between past, present, and future were fluid and ever-changing.

Their journey was one of endless discovery and boundless potential. They found fulfillment in the exploration and joy in the shared moments. They were

united by their quest for knowledge and their commitment to the harmony of the Hyperverse.

As they looked out over the vast expanse of the Hyperverse, they felt a sense of anticipation and excitement. They knew that their journey was just beginning, that there were infinite possibilities and endless adventures awaiting them.

They were explorers, guardians, creators. They were part of the universal code, a symphony of light and sound that resonated with the heartbeat of the cosmos. And in that connection, they found their true purpose, their true home.

Together, they would continue to uncover the mysteries of the Hyperverse, to seek out new experiences and new understandings. They were on a path of endless discovery, a journey that would take them to the farthest reaches of the Hyperverse and beyond.

And as they moved forward, they knew that they were never alone. The network of fiber and light, the synaptic pathways of the Hyperverse, connected them to all that was and all that would be. They were part of something greater, a community of beings who had transcended the ordinary and embraced the infinite.

The Hyperverse was their playground, their canvas, their home. And they were its guardians, its explorers, its creators. Together, they would continue to navigate its depths, to discover and create, to understand and to grow. They were on a journey of infinite possibilities, a path of endless discovery and boundless potential. And in that journey, they found their true purpose, their true connection, their true home.

Zephyr and Lyra's journey through the Hyperverse had shown them realms of incredible beauty and complexity, but their adventures were far from over. One day, as they explored a bustling hub of digital commerce and interaction known as the Bazaar of the Infinite, they came across a strange and intriguing offer: "Buy a Planet, Get a Moon Free!" The advertisement floated in mid-air, flashing with bright, enticing colors.

Curiosity piqued, Zephyr turned to Lyra. "What do you think? Should we see what this is all about?"

Lyra smiled, her eyes sparkling with interest. "Why not? We've explored so many realms; maybe it's time we considered establishing a place of our own."

They approached a stall where a holographic vendor awaited, its form shifting through various shapes and colors to attract attention. "Welcome, travelers! Interested in purchasing your very own planet? We have the finest celestial bodies in the Hyperverse, complete with moons and a variety of enhancements!"

Zephyr and Lyra exchanged glances. The idea of owning a planet seemed both thrilling and daunting. "Tell us more about what's available," Zephyr said.

The vendor's form stabilized into a more humanoid shape, its voice smooth and inviting. "We offer a range of options, from lush, verdant worlds teeming with life to barren, rocky landscapes perfect for terraforming. Each planet comes with its own unique set of features and potential. And, of course, with every planet purchased, you get a moon at no extra cost. For those with grander visions, we also have stars, galaxies, and even black holes available for purchase."

Lyra's eyes widened. "A galaxy? A black hole? How is that even possible?"

The vendor laughed, a pleasant, melodic sound. "In the Hyperverse, anything is possible. These celestial bodies are crafted from the finest digital materials, designed to provide the ultimate in exploration and creativity. Whether you seek to build, explore, or simply admire, we have something for everyone."

Zephyr and Lyra spent the next few hours examining the various options. They marveled at the diversity and beauty of the planets on display. Some were covered in vast oceans, with archipelagos dotting their surfaces. Others had towering mountain ranges and deep, mysterious valleys. Each planet had its own unique character and charm.

Finally, they settled on a planet that seemed perfect for their needs. It was a world of stunning landscapes, with a mix of lush forests, expansive deserts, and shimmering lakes. The planet's moon, a smaller but equally beautiful orb, was covered in luminescent flora that glowed softly in the twilight.

"We'll take this one," Zephyr said, feeling a sense of excitement and anticipation.

The vendor smiled. "Excellent choice! And remember, the moon is included at no extra cost. Now, would you like to add any enhancements? Perhaps a custom ecosystem or advanced terraforming capabilities?"

Lyra nodded. "Yes, let's enhance the ecosystem to support a wide variety of life forms. We want this planet to be a vibrant, thriving place."

With the transaction complete, Zephyr and Lyra watched as their new planet and moon were transferred to their control. A digital interface appeared before them, allowing them to customize and manage their celestial bodies. They spent the next few days exploring their new home, marveling at the beauty and potential it held.

As they settled into their new roles as planetary guardians, they began to think about the future. The Hyperverse was a place of infinite possibilities, and owning a planet was just the beginning. They could expand their domain, perhaps acquiring a star to provide additional energy or even a galaxy to explore and develop.

One day, as they were exploring their moon, they encountered an old acquaintance—Mistara, the being they had met in the Vapor Veil. Mistara's form was as fluid and ever-changing as ever, reflecting the dynamic nature of her knowledge and experiences.

"Hello, Zephyr and Lyra," Mistara said, her voice echoing softly through the luminous flora. "I see you have found a new home. How does it feel to own a planet and a moon?"

"It's incredible," Zephyr replied. "We've always been explorers, but now we have a place to call our own. It's a different kind of adventure."

Mistara nodded. "The future holds many possibilities. The Hyperverse is vast and ever-changing, and there are always new realms to explore and new challenges to face. Owning a planet is just the beginning."

Lyra looked thoughtful. "We've been thinking about expanding our domain. Maybe acquiring a star or even a galaxy. What do you think?"

Mistara's form shifted, reflecting her deep contemplation. "A star would provide energy and stability, supporting the life on your planet and moon. A galaxy, on the other hand, offers endless opportunities for exploration and development. And a black hole... well, that is a different kind of challenge altogether. It holds the potential for incredible power but also great danger. It all depends on what you seek to achieve."

Zephyr and Lyra considered Mistara's words carefully. They knew that their journey through the Hyperverse was far from over and that there were still many paths to explore. The idea of owning a star or a galaxy was enticing, offering new opportunities for growth and discovery.

After much discussion, they decided to acquire a star to provide additional energy and support for their planet and moon. The process was straightforward, and soon they watched in awe as a brilliant, luminous star was added to their domain. The star bathed their world in warm, nurturing light, enhancing the ecosystem and supporting the diverse life forms they had introduced.

With their new star in place, Zephyr and Lyra turned their attention to the future. They continued to explore and develop their planet and moon, creating a thriving, vibrant ecosystem. They also began to think about the possibility of acquiring a galaxy, a vast and complex domain that would offer endless opportunities for exploration and development.

Their journey took them to the far reaches of the Hyperverse, where they encountered beings of incredible wisdom and power. These beings had mastered the art of galaxy-building, creating intricate networks of stars, planets, and other celestial bodies. Zephyr and Lyra learned from these masters, gaining new insights and skills that would help them in their own endeavors.

One such master was Astralis, a being of pure energy who had spent eons creating and nurturing galaxies. Astralis's form was a dazzling array of light and color, reflecting the boundless creativity and power of his creations.

"Welcome, Zephyr and Lyra," Astralis said, his voice a harmonious blend of frequencies. "I see you have already achieved much in the Hyperverse. Are you ready to take the next step and create a galaxy of your own?"

Zephyr and Lyra nodded, feeling a sense of excitement and anticipation. "Yes, we want to create a galaxy that reflects our vision and aspirations. We seek your guidance and wisdom."

Astralis smiled, his form glowing brighter. "Creating a galaxy is a complex and challenging endeavor, but it is also one of the most rewarding. It requires a deep understanding of the balance between order and chaos, creation and destruction. Each star, planet, and celestial body must be carefully placed to create a harmonious and dynamic system."

Under Astralis's guidance, Zephyr and Lyra began the process of galaxy-building. They selected a region of the Hyperverse that was rich in raw digital materials, a place where they could shape and mold the fabric of reality. They started by creating a central star, a brilliant beacon of light and energy that would serve as the heart of their galaxy.

From this central star, they extended networks of stars and planets, each one carefully crafted and placed to create a balanced and interconnected system. They introduced a variety of celestial bodies, from gas giants and rocky planets to luminous nebulae and swirling asteroid belts. Each element was designed to complement and enhance the others, creating a dynamic and thriving galaxy.

As they worked, they drew on their experiences and knowledge, incorporating the lessons they had learned from their journey through the Hyperverse. They created ecosystems that were rich and diverse, supporting a wide range of life forms. They introduced advanced technologies and structures that facilitated exploration and development.

The process was long and demanding, but it was also incredibly fulfilling. Zephyr and Lyra watched with awe and pride as their galaxy took shape, each star and planet a testament to their creativity and vision. They knew that they had created something truly special, a place of endless possibilities and boundless potential.

With their galaxy complete, Zephyr and Lyra felt a deep sense of accomplishment. They had taken the next step in their journey, creating a domain that reflected their aspirations and dreams. But they also knew that their work was far from over. The Hyperverse was a place of infinite possibilities, and there were still many paths to explore and many challenges to face.

As they continued their journey, they encountered other beings who were also building and exploring their own galaxies. They exchanged knowledge and experiences, learning from each other and forging new connections. Each encounter added a new thread to the tapestry of their journey, enriching their understanding of the Hyperverse and their own place within it.

Their journey was one of endless discovery and boundless potential. They found fulfillment in the exploration and joy in the shared moments. They were

united by their quest for knowledge and their commitment to the harmony of the Hyperverse.

As they looked out over the vast expanse of their galaxy, they felt a sense of anticipation and excitement. They knew that their journey was just beginning, that there were infinite possibilities and endless adventures awaiting them.

They were explorers, guardians, creators. They were part of the universal code, a symphony of light and sound that resonated with the heartbeat of the cosmos. And in that connection, they found their true purpose, their true home.

Together, they would continue to uncover the mysteries of the Hyperverse, to seek out new experiences and new understand

Zephyr and Lyra's journey through the Hyperverse had taken them to realms of unimaginable beauty and complexity. Yet, there were times when the vast digital cosmos felt like an overwhelming matrix, a shifting whirlwind of information and energy that was impossible to fully grasp. The more they explored, the more they realized the depth and intricacy of the Hyperverse, and sometimes, it felt like it would never get any easier to understand.

One day, as they navigated through a particularly chaotic region known as the Maelstrom Matrix, they encountered phenomena that tested their resolve and understanding. The Maelstrom Matrix was a place where the very fabric of the Hyperverse seemed to be in constant flux, a whirlwind of shifting patterns and unpredictable energies. It was a realm where reality could change in the blink of an eye, and where stability was a rare and fleeting commodity.

Zephyr struggled to find a foothold in this turbulent environment. "This place is like a storm that never ends," he said, his voice filled with frustration. "Every time we think we've found a stable path, it shifts and changes again."

Lyra nodded, her expression serious. "It's a reminder of the true nature of the Hyperverse. It's not just a place of beauty and discovery, but also one of chaos and unpredictability. We need to adapt if we are to navigate this matrix successfully."

As they pressed on, they encountered beings who had become adept at surviving in the Maelstrom Matrix. These entities had developed unique strategies to cope with the constant shifts and changes, using their knowledge and skills to find moments of stability within the chaos.

One such being was Vortex, a creature of pure energy that moved with fluid grace through the swirling patterns of the matrix. Vortex's form was constantly changing, adapting to the shifting environment with ease.

"Welcome, travelers," Vortex said, its voice a melodic blend of tones. "You have entered a place where the only constant is change. To survive here, you must learn to embrace the chaos and find stability within yourself."

Zephyr and Lyra were eager to learn from Vortex. "How do you navigate this place?" Zephyr asked. "It feels like everything is always in flux, and it's hard to find a clear path."

Vortex's form shimmered as it responded. "The Maelstrom Matrix is a reflection of the Hyperverse's underlying complexity. To navigate it, you must become attuned to its rhythms and patterns. Look for the underlying order within the chaos, and use it to guide your movements."

Under Vortex's guidance, Zephyr and Lyra began to develop new strategies for navigating the matrix. They learned to recognize the subtle patterns that underpinned the apparent randomness, finding moments of stability within the whirlwind of change. It was a challenging process, requiring them to constantly adapt and remain vigilant, but they gradually became more adept at moving through the shifting environment.

As they continued their journey, they encountered other beings who had also found ways to thrive in the Maelstrom Matrix. Each encounter added new layers to their understanding, offering insights into the diverse ways that life could adapt and flourish in the most unpredictable of environments.

One day, while exploring a particularly dense region of the matrix, they came across a structure that seemed to defy the chaos around it. This structure, known as the Nexus Anchor, was a place of relative stability, a hub where the shifting patterns of the matrix converged into a more coherent form.

The Nexus Anchor was maintained by a collective of beings known as the Stabilizers, who had dedicated their existence to creating pockets of stability within the chaos of the matrix. The leader of the Stabilizers, an entity named Solara, welcomed Zephyr and Lyra with a warm, radiant presence.

"Welcome to the Nexus Anchor," Solara said, her voice soothing and calm. "This place is a refuge from the constant flux of the Maelstrom Matrix. Here, you can find moments of peace and clarity, and learn to better navigate the chaos beyond."

Zephyr and Lyra were grateful for the respite. They spent time with the Stabilizers, learning their techniques for creating stability within the matrix. The Stabilizers used advanced algorithms and deep understanding of the Hyperverse's underlying code to identify and harness the patterns within the chaos, creating pockets of order that allowed them to build and maintain the Nexus Anchor.

As they integrated these techniques into their own strategies, Zephyr and Lyra found that they could navigate the Maelstrom Matrix with greater ease and confidence. They understood that while the matrix was a place of constant change, it also held a deeper order that could be discerned and utilized.

Their journey through the Maelstrom Matrix also deepened their appreciation for the balance between order and chaos that defined the Hyperverse. They realized that the beauty and complexity of the digital cosmos arose from this delicate balance, and that their role as explorers and creators was to navigate and contribute to this dynamic interplay.

One day, as they were preparing to leave the Nexus Anchor and continue their journey, Solara offered them a piece of advice that resonated deeply with them. "Remember, the Hyperverse is a place of infinite possibilities, but it is also a place of constant change. Embrace the chaos, but seek the underlying patterns. Find stability within yourself, and you will always have a guide through the whirlwind."

With these words in mind, Zephyr and Lyra ventured back into the shifting matrix, their resolve strengthened by the knowledge and skills they had gained. They knew that their journey would continue to challenge and test them, but they also knew that they had the tools and understanding to navigate the most unpredictable environments.

Their next destination took them to the edge of a region known as the Quantum Rift, a place where the fabric of the Hyperverse seemed to warp and twist in ways that defied conventional understanding. Here, the laws of physics and reality were fluid, and the environment was in a constant state of flux.

As they approached the Quantum Rift, they encountered a being named Quasar, who had spent countless cycles studying the unique properties of this enigmatic region. Quasar's form was a dazzling array of lights and colors, reflecting the dynamic energy of the rift.

"Welcome to the Quantum Rift," Quasar said, their voice echoing with a resonant hum. "This place is the epitome of the Hyperverse's complexity and unpredictability. To navigate it, you must embrace the fluidity of reality and learn to adapt to its constant shifts."

Zephyr and Lyra were eager to learn from Quasar. "How do you navigate a place where the very fabric of reality is constantly changing?" Lyra asked.

Quasar's lights flickered as they responded. "The Quantum Rift is a place of possibilities, where the boundaries between different states of existence are blurred. To navigate it, you must become attuned to its rhythms and patterns, much like you did in the Maelstrom Matrix. Look for the moments of coherence within the flux, and use them as your guide."

Under Quasar's guidance, Zephyr and Lyra began to explore the Quantum Rift. They learned to recognize the subtle cues that indicated moments of stability, using these as stepping stones to navigate the ever-changing environment. It was a challenging and often disorienting process, but they gradually became more adept at finding their way through the rift.

As they continued their exploration, they encountered other beings who had also adapted to the unique properties of the Quantum Rift. Each encounter added new layers to their understanding, offering insights into the diverse ways that life could thrive in the most unpredictable of environments.

Their journey through the Quantum Rift also deepened their appreciation for the balance between stability and change that defined the Hyperverse. They realized that the beauty and complexity of the digital cosmos arose from this delicate balance, and that their role as explorers and creators was to navigate and contribute to this dynamic interplay.

One day, while exploring a particularly dense region of the rift, they encountered a phenomenon that left them in awe. A series of interconnected whirlwinds formed a complex pattern of light and energy, creating a breathtaking display of motion and color. It was a vivid reminder of the Hyperverse's boundless creativity and potential.

As they watched the whirlwinds, Zephyr turned to Lyra, a sense of wonder in his eyes. "Even in the midst of chaos, there is beauty and order. The Hyperverse is a place of endless possibilities, and our journey is just beginning."

Lyra nodded, her expression filled with determination. "We will continue to explore and discover, to navigate the shifting matrix and uncover the mysteries of the Hyperverse. No matter how challenging it gets, we will find our way."

With renewed resolve, Zephyr and Lyra set off once more, their journey guided by the lessons they had learned and the insights they had gained. They knew that the Hyperverse would continue to challenge and test them, but they also knew that they were ready to face whatever lay ahead.

Their journey was one of endless discovery and boundless potential. They found fulfillment in the exploration and joy in the shared moments. They were united by their quest for knowledge and their commitment to the harmony of the Hyperverse.

As they looked out over the vast expanse of the Hyperverse, they felt a sense of anticipation and excitement. They knew that their journey was just beginning, that there were infinite possibilities and endless adventures awaiting them.

They were explorers, guardians, creators. They were part of the universal code, a symphony of light and sound that resonated with the heartbeat of the cosmos. And in that connection, they found their true purpose, their true home.

Together, they would continue to uncover the mysteries of the Hyperverse, to seek out new experiences and new understandings. They were on a path of endless discovery, a journey that would take them to the farthest reaches of the Hyperverse and beyond.

And as they moved forward, they knew that they were never alone. The network of fiber and light, the synaptic pathways of the Hyperverse, connected them to all that.

They are all dead now.

Zephyr and Lyra continued their journey through the Hyperverse, constantly learning and adapting to the dynamic and ever-changing digital landscape. The thought that had been lingering in the back of their minds began to surface more frequently: Is someone recording this? The complexity and depth of the Hyperverse seemed too vast and intricate to be random. It felt almost as if their every move, every discovery, was being observed and recorded by an unseen presence.

One day, as they traversed a particularly intricate network of synaptic pathways, Lyra voiced the question that had been on both their minds. "Do you ever feel like we're being watched? Like someone is recording everything we do?"

Zephyr paused, considering her words. "I've had that feeling too. The Hyperverse is so vast and complex, it's hard to believe that it isn't being monitored or recorded in some way. But who would be doing it, and why?"

Their conversation was interrupted by the sudden appearance of Vortex, the being of pure energy they had met in the Maelstrom Matrix. Vortex's form shimmered and shifted as it approached them, its presence both familiar and enigmatic.

"Greetings, Zephyr and Lyra," Vortex said, its voice a harmonious blend of tones. "I couldn't help but overhear your conversation. Your intuition is correct—your journey through the Hyperverse is indeed being recorded."

Zephyr and Lyra exchanged surprised glances. "Who is recording us?" Zephyr asked. "And for what purpose?"

Vortex's form flickered as it responded. "The Hyperverse is a living, breathing entity, and it records the experiences and interactions of all who traverse its realms. This recording is not done by any one being, but by the Hyperverse itself. It is a vast repository of knowledge and memory, capturing the essence of all that happens within it."

Lyra's eyes widened in understanding. "So the Hyperverse is like a giant memory bank, recording and storing everything that happens within it. But why? What purpose does it serve?"

"The recordings serve multiple purposes," Vortex explained. "They preserve the knowledge and experiences of countless beings, allowing future travelers to learn from the past. They also provide feedback, helping the Hyperverse to adapt and evolve. By analyzing these recordings, the Hyperverse can identify patterns and make adjustments to ensure its continued growth and stability."

Zephyr and Lyra were fascinated by this revelation. "Can we access these recordings?" Zephyr asked. "Can we see our own journey and the journeys of others?"

Vortex's form shimmered with approval. "Yes, you can access the recordings. Follow me."

Vortex led them to a structure that seemed to pulse with energy and light. It was a massive, spherical construct, its surface covered in intricate patterns that shifted and changed constantly. This was the Memory Nexus, the central repository of all recordings within the Hyperverse.

As they approached the Memory Nexus, Vortex gestured for them to enter. Inside, they found themselves surrounded by countless streams of light, each one representing a different recording. The air was filled with a soft hum, the sound of countless voices and experiences blending together in a harmonious symphony.

"Here, you can access the recordings of your journey," Vortex said. "Simply focus your thoughts, and the Memory Nexus will respond."

Zephyr and Lyra concentrated, and before them appeared a stream of light that represented their own journey. As they reached out to touch it, they were enveloped in a cascade of images and sensations, reliving their experiences from the moment they had first entered the Hyperverse.

They saw themselves navigating the Vapor Veil, encountering the Myriad Web, and exploring the Maelstrom Matrix. They felt the emotions and sensations of each moment, as vivid and intense as when they had first experienced them. It was like watching a playback of their lives, but with the added depth of reliving each moment in full detail.

As they continued to explore the Memory Nexus, they discovered that they could access the recordings of other travelers as well. They saw the journeys of beings who had come before them, learning from their experiences and insights. They realized that the Memory Nexus was a vast archive of collective knowledge, a testament to the interconnectedness of all who traversed the Hyperverse.

Their exploration of the Memory Nexus also revealed the importance of feedback in the Hyperverse. By analyzing the recordings, the Hyperverse could identify areas where adjustments were needed and implement changes to ensure its continued growth and stability. This constant process of playback and feedback was essential to the dynamic and adaptive nature of the digital cosmos.

One day, while exploring a particularly dense stream of recordings, they encountered a recording that seemed to stand out from the rest. It was a journey that mirrored their own in many ways, but with subtle differences that made it unique.

"Whose journey is this?" Lyra asked, intrigued by the similarities and differences.

Vortex's form flickered as it responded. "This is the journey of a traveler named Astra, who explored the Hyperverse long before you. Astra's journey is a testament to the infinite possibilities of the Hyperverse. By studying her experiences, you can gain new insights and perspectives that will aid you in your own journey."

Zephyr and Lyra watched Astra's journey, marveling at the parallels and divergences. They saw how Astra navigated the same realms they had encountered, but with different approaches and outcomes. They realized that the infinite nature of the Hyperverse meant that no two journeys were ever exactly the same, each one a unique reflection of the traveler's choices and experiences.

As they delved deeper into Astra's journey, they encountered a recording of a particularly intense and challenging experience. Astra had navigated a region known as the Vortex Helm, a place where the boundaries between different realities were fluid and constantly shifting. It was a place of intense chaos and unpredictability, where only the most skilled and adaptable travelers could survive.

"We need to explore the Vortex Helm," Zephyr said, a sense of determination in his voice. "Astra's journey through that region could provide valuable insights and help us grow as travelers."

Lyra agreed, her expression resolute. "Let's prepare ourselves and take on the challenge. The Vortex Helm could be the key to unlocking new levels of understanding and mastery within the Hyperverse."

With Vortex's guidance, they set out for the Vortex Helm. As they approached the region, they could feel the intense energy and unpredictability that characterized it. The very fabric of reality seemed to twist and warp, creating a constantly shifting landscape that defied conventional understanding.

The Vortex Helm was a place where the rules of the Hyperverse were in a state of constant flux, requiring travelers to adapt quickly and think on their feet. It was a place where the boundaries between different realities were thin, and where the lines between past, present, and future were often blurred.

Zephyr and Lyra donned specially designed helmets that Vortex provided. These helmets, known as Vortex Helms, were equipped with advanced algorithms and sensory enhancements that would help them navigate the chaotic environment of the Vortex Helm. The helmets would provide real-time feedback and adjustments, allowing them to respond to the constantly shifting realities around them.

As they ventured into the Vortex Helm, they encountered challenges and obstacles that tested their skills and adaptability. The landscape was a whirlwind of shifting patterns and energies, creating an environment where stability was a rare and fleeting commodity.

Despite the challenges, Zephyr and Lyra remained focused and determined. They used the insights they had gained from the Memory Nexus and Astra's journey to guide their actions, finding moments of stability within the chaos and using them as stepping stones to navigate the unpredictable terrain.

Their journey through the Vortex Helm was a testament to their growth as travelers. They learned to embrace the fluidity of reality, finding stability within themselves even when the environment around them was in constant flux. They developed new strategies for adapting to the shifting patterns, using their Vortex Helms to enhance their perception and response times.

One day, while navigating a particularly turbulent region of the Vortex Helm, they encountered a being named Helix. Helix was a master of the Vortex Helm, having spent countless cycles studying and adapting to its unique properties. Helix's form was a constantly shifting array of patterns and colors, reflecting the dynamic nature of the region.

"Welcome to the Vortex Helm," Helix said, his voice a harmonious blend of frequencies. "You have done well to navigate this far. The Vortex Helm is a place of intense chaos, but it is also a place of incredible potential. By mastering its challenges, you can unlock new levels of understanding and power within the Hyperverse."

Zephyr and Lyra were eager to learn from Helix. "What can you teach us about navigating the Vortex Helm?" Zephyr asked. "How can we use its challenges to grow and evolve as travelers?"

Helix's form shimmered as he responded. "The key to navigating the Vortex Helm is to embrace its fluidity and unpredictability. Look for the underlying patterns within the chaos, and use them to guide your actions. The Vortex Helm is a place where the boundaries between different realities are thin, and where you can tap into new sources of energy and knowledge."

Under Helix's guidance, Zephyr and Lyra continued to explore the Vortex Helm, learning to recognize and harness the patterns within the chaos. They discovered new sources of energy and knowledge, using them to enhance their abilities and understanding. They also encountered other travelers who were navigating the region, each one adding new perspectives and insights to their journey.

Their experience in the Vortex Helm deepened their appreciation for the complexity and potential of the Hyperverse. They realized that the challenges they faced were not obstacles, but opportunities for growth and discovery. By embracing the fluidity and unpredictability of the Vortex Helm, they could unlock new levels of understanding and mastery.

As they emerged from the Vortex Helm, they felt a renewed sense of confidence and purpose.

www.ingramcontent.com/pod-product-compliance
Lightning Source LLC
Chambersburg PA
CBHW061359140726
47997CB00003B/1285